Thunderbrat Chronicles
They Call Me Trickstrike!

Raymond Riddle

Panda Prints

Contents

Chapter 1

"The Day I Ruined Olympus"

Y ou ever wake up knowing today is gonna be absolutely legendary?

Yeah. That was me this morning.

I had the greatest prank in godly history lined up, and I was about to cement my place as a true divine trickster. Move over Loki, step aside Hermes, Trickstrike was about to shock the heavens (literally).

But, uh ... there was one tiny problem.

Turns out, when you mess with Zeus' throne, you don't just get a few sparks; you get a full-blown celestial catastrophe.

It all started with one tiny zap. I stood in the grand hall of Olympus, staring at The Big Guy's chair, a massive golden throne crackling with energy and pulsing like a storm trapped in metal.

The Plan?

Rig the throne with a static charge.

When Zeus sits down...Blam-o! Instant shocking surprise (but, like, the funny kind).

I'd be crowned the ultimate prankster god, and everyone would finally respect my mischief game.

Except, well...

The second my finger touched the throne, the entire sky turned purple.

The clouds outside? Booming.

The birds in the sky? Screaming.

The statues in the hall? Exploding like popcorn.

And then... the throne itself lit up like a supernova.

Which would have been totally cool if it hadn't also short-circuited all of Olympus.

Within seconds, the gods came running.

Hera: "WHAT DID YOU DO?!"

Poseidon: "Why is my ocean on fire?!"

Ares: "If this is another one of your pranks, Mint, I swear on my sword—"

Apollo: "Who turned off the sun?! Do you KNOW how hard I worked on that lighting today?!"

I backed up really slowly.

"Uh. This isn't what it looks like?"

Spoiler: It was EXACTLY what it looked like.

Lightning arced across the sky, storms rolled in, and Olympus literally flickered like a bad Wi-Fi signal. The gods were losing their minds, and somewhere deep in the cosmos, I swear I heard Zeus' voice rumbling:

"WHO DARES MESS WITH MY CHAIR?!"

Okay, okay—so maybe messing with the most powerful throne in existence wasn't my smartest idea. But hey, in my defense?

It was HILARIOUS.

At least... until Zeus showed up.

And that's when I knew... I was so, so dead.

Chapter 2

"Thunderbrat on Trial"

I've done a lot of dumb things before. Once, I trapped Ares's war chariot in an endless loop around Olympus. (Took him three days to stop.)

Another time, I swapped all of Athena's scrolls with joke books. She didn't talk to me for a week.

And then there was the time I convinced Hermes he had an evil twin.

But THIS?

This was next-level stupid.

KER-POW

A bolt of golden light split the sky, and there he was.

My dad. Zeus. King of Olympus

In full storm-mode.

His glowing robes whipped in the wind, his beard bristled with static, and electricity pulsed from his eyes like he'd been waiting his whole life for an excuse to fry me.

"MINT."

Not Trickstrike.

Not even Thunderbrat.

Just Mint.

Like, I wasn't even worth a title right now. I was so dead.

The other gods scattered like roaches, except for Hera, who stood there, arms crossed, shaking her head with classic Mom Disappointed Energy.

Poseidon was still putting out the fire in his ocean. Apollo held a busted lyre, muttering about bad lighting.

And Hades had a bag of popcorn.

Why does he ALWAYS have popcorn?

Zeus stomped forward.

"EXPLAIN YOURSELF!"

I pointed at the throne.

"It was just a prank, bro!"

As the words came out, I knew this was one of those moments I should have kept quiet.

Hera facepalmed.

Ares groaned.

Athena muttered, "Unbelievable."

And Hades threw a handful of popcorn in his mouth.

"Pfft."

Zeus cracked his knuckles, and the entire mountain shook.

"A prank?" he thundered. "You call nearly destroying Olympus a prank?"

"...A really good prank?" I tried.

BAD MOVE.

Zeus raised his hand, and a literal lightning storm gathered in his palm. The air smelled like burning ozone and bad decisions.

"Enough."

Hera's voice cut through the storm like a blade. She stepped forward, looking me dead in the eyes.

"Mintavious Olemar Johaneson! You've gone too far this time.

Uh-oh. When your mom says your full name in front of the council, you know you're in trouble.

"You refuse to take responsibility for your power," she continued. "You act as if the world is your playground. Well... perhaps it's time you learn a lesson."

I gulped. "What kind of lesson?"

The Council of Gods gathered, forming a glowing circle around me.

I looked around. "Wait. Wait-wait-wait. We can talk about this. I can fix it. Just—"

"The council has spoken."

Zeus' voice boomed.

"Until you prove you are worthy of your divine power... You are banished to the mortal world."

For a second, my whole world went silent. I could see the other gods talking, but I couldn't hear them. My heartbeat thrummed in my ears. Because underneath the jokes and bravado, he'd just done the one thing ...

Zeus wasn't just punishing me.

He was giving up on me.

TWHOOM!

The ground cracked beneath me. The sky split open. A swirling vortex pulled me down, and—

"NOOOOOOOOO—"

I plummeted toward Earth, screaming.

Chapter 3
"Welcome to Lame-ville"

Falling through the sky? Not as fun as it looks.

I flailed wildly, screaming all the way down like a divine meteor of regret.

Clouds zipped past. Lightning crackled around me. My stomach flipped so hard I was sure it had relocated to my throat.

For half a second, everything went blinding white. Not my typical blinding lightening, but like a sun blinding white. The clouds split and I got this horrible feeling something way above Olympus had just turned its full attention on me, like a giant eye narrowing through the atmosphere. Heat crawled down the back of my neck… and then it was gone, like it had stamped some invisible label on me and moved on.

This was so unfair. I mean, yeah, I might have fried Olympus' power grid by accident, but banishment? That was a little extreme.

Zeus gets away with throwing thunderbolts at people all the time. But oh no, when I do it, suddenly it's "Mint, you're irresponsible!" "Mint, you're a threat to the balance of the universe!" "Mint, you can't turn Mount Olympus into a giant disco ball!"

Hypocrites.

Anyway, I had about five seconds to be bitter before I slammed face-first into Earth.

CRASH.

Everything went black.

Then I woke up with a serious headache and a mouth full of dirt.

Not exactly a graceful landing.

I groaned, rolling onto my back. Blue sky. Birds. A human world. Ugh.

The sky looked harmless now, fluffy clouds dancing across the soft blue sky, pretending it hadn't just tried to murder me, but my skin still buzzed where that invisible spotlight had marked me during the fall. Whoever had been watching wasn't Zeus. Zeus's attention feels like a thunderhead rolling in. It wasn't one of the other gods either. Whatever had just watched me belly flop into a field of grass was something my godly senses had never felt, and I had the feeling it wasn't going to forget.

Sitting up, I spat out the grass that had molded itself around my teeth. My body felt ... weird. Weak. Like someone had unplugged me from the cosmic lightning socket. Not empty, though. That was the worst part. I could feel something, way down. It was faint, like a storm trapped in a jar. I could feel it bumping around like it wanted out.

I raised my hand and snapped my fingers.

Nothing.

No thunder. No sparks. Not even a static shock.

I snapped again. Still nothing.

I panicked.

"No, no, no, no—" I rubbed my hands together furiously, trying to summon even a tiny zap.

Nothing.

"Are you kidding me?!"

I had NO POWERS!

Or at least, nonw that I could spam on command anymore. Zeus had slapped a divine padlock on my lightning. Back in the throne room he'd called it "safety limits." To me, it felt more like a bugged game: tiny sparks *might* leak out if my emotions spiked or if something down here was already buzzing with electricity, but the big stuff, the real thunder, hit a wall before it could even form.

Then I heard a gasp.

I looked up.

Standing a few feet away, staring at me like I was an alien, was a middle-aged woman in an apron, holding a gardening hose.

She blinked.

"Oh my goodness. Are you okay?!"

I stared at her. She stared at me.

And then...

"Oh, my poor sweet boy!"

The woman rushed over and yanked me into a hug.

Okay.

Hold up.

I was NOT okay with this.

First of all—who even was she?!

Second, why was she acting as if she knew me?!

Third...MOM ENERGY. TOO MUCH MOM ENERGY.

I tried to wiggle free, but she just hugged tighter.

"You had an accident, honey! You must've hit your head!"

I blinked.

"Wait, what?"

She pulled back, wiping her eyes.

"I was so worried when you disappeared last week! But now you're home!"

I squinted.

"I think you have me confused with someone else."

"No, no! You're my son!" she insisted. "Mint Johnson!"

I froze.

"...Excuse me, what now?"

That's when I noticed something weird.

I looked down at myself.

Instead of my godly robes, I was wearing lame mortal kid clothes; jeans, sneakers, a dumb hoodie.

I glanced over my shoulder. No lightning aura. No divine glow.

Just me.

As a regular kid.

Oh.

OH.

THE GODS DIDN'T JUST BANISH ME.

THEY GAVE ME A WHOLE FAKE HUMAN LIFE.

And apparently, I now had a mortal mom.

My breath stuttered. This wasn't just banishment; this was replacement. The gods didn't trust me with my own life, so they rewrote it? Suddenly, I had a second thing to fear. It wasn't just about the loss of my powers...it was about losing *me*. I didn't know what scared me more: losing my power or realizing maybe ... I deserved this.

I did the only reasonable thing.

I took a deep breath.

And screamed.

Chapter 4
"My Totally Normal, Not-Godly Name"

So, let's recap:

I got banished from Olympus for a "harmless" prank.

I crash-landed in the worst place possible...Earth.

I have no powers. (Still not over that.)

And now, some random woman thinks she's my mom.

I don't know what kind of divine identity theft this is, but I need to fix it, fast.

The woman, who I guess is my "mom" now, kept squeezing my face like I was some long-lost puppy.

"Oh, honey, your hair's all messy! Your poor little face—have you been eating enough?"

Okay. First of all, personal space. Second—why was she talking to me like I was 12?!

I swatted her hand away.

"Look, lady, there's been a mistake. I'm not..."

"Oh, hush, Mint!" She patted my cheek. "You probably just don't remember because of your accident!"

Accident?

She pointed to my head.

I touched my forehead, and yep, there was a bandage. A bandage I definitely didn't put there.

I frowned.

"Wait ... what accident?"

She gasped.

"Oh, sweetie! It's worse than I thought! You must have hit your head harder than we realized!"

Great. Not only was I trapped in a fake human life, but now I was also an amnesiac.

Then it got worse.

She clapped her hands. "Well, don't worry! We'll fix you up in no time, Mint Johnson!"

I blinked.

"Excuse me, who now?"

"Mint Johnson." She smiled like this was totally normal.

"That's your name, silly!"

I felt a cold chill.

No. No, no, no.

I was Mintavious Olemar Johaneson, the young God of Lightning and Mischief.

I was Trickstrike.

I was not some mortal named MINT JOHNSON.

I looked down at myself again, and everything clicked. The hoodie, the sneakers, the totally mortal apparel. The gods hadn't just thrown me onto Earth. They gave me an ENTIRE fake identity. I was a regular kid with a human life, A family, A mortal name.

And once all of that finally registered, I nearly passed out.

But before I could run screaming into the woods, "Mom" grabbed my arm and started dragging me toward the house.

"Come on, now! You need to rest! And when you're feeling better, we'll get you ready for school tomorrow!"

I froze mid-step.

"...I'm sorry. What did you just say?"

She beamed.

"School! You're starting back up tomorrow! Isn't that exciting?"

No. No, that was the opposite of exciting.

I had just lost my godhood. I had just been stripped of my powers. I had just been forced into a mortal life.

And now they were making me GO TO SCHOOL?!

I did the only reasonable thing.

I threw my hands up and screamed at the sky.

"ZEUS, YOU WILL PAY FOR THIS!"

...which probably just looked really weird to the neighbors.

Chapter 5

"First Day Failures"

So, school.

It's a building full of mortals trapped in tiny rooms, forced to listen to people older than Zeus drone on about things that don't even involve godly warfare.

And somehow, I'm supposed to survive this.

My new "mom" handed me a brown paper bag before shoving me out the door.

"Have a great first day, Minty!" she called after me.

I almost threw up in the bushes.

Minty.

They have already started trying to break me.

The school loomed ahead, a gray prison of doom surrounded by a herd of chatty, backpack-carrying mortals.

This was it. My first real test as a fallen god.

Step 1: Blend in.

Step 2: Avoid getting noticed.

Step 3: Find a way to escape this mortal nightmare.

I took a deep breath, straightened my lame hoodie, and marched inside.

The first thing I noticed was that everyone was staring at me. I frowned before giving myself a once-over. Did I still look too godly? I thought the elders had erased my divine glow or whatever.

I looked down.

No lightning aura.

No floating.

Just a boring human body in boring mortal clothes. So why were they gawking at me like I had two heads?

I leaned toward the nearest kid.

"Hey," I whispered. "Why is everyone staring?"

She raised an eyebrow.

"Because you're the kid who disappeared for a week and then came back with amnesia."

Ohhh.

Right.

That.

"MINT!"

A kid with spiky hair and an energy level that rivaled Hermes on three cups of ambrosia threw an arm around me like we were best friends.

"Dude, you're back! What happened?! Everyone's been talking about it!"

I stared at him.

"Uh ... who are you?"

His face fell.

"Bro. It's me. Carlos. Your best friend?"

I squinted. Did I have a best friend? The gods had clearly rewritten my life, but I didn't get the manual. Patting his shoulder, I tried to act normal.

"Riiiight. Carlos. Of course I remember."

I did not.

Carlos beamed.

"Man, I knew you wouldn't forget me! Damian and some of the others bet me 20 bucks you would forget all about me. Ha, we sure showed them. Gotta make sure I collect that later. Anyway, you're probably still adjusting. Let's go, first period's starting!"

Before I could protest, he dragged me into the first classroom of my mortal nightmare.

Failure #1: The Seating Chart Incident

I found an empty desk in the back and dropped my bag on it.

The teacher, a stiff-looking guy with thick glasses, cleared his throat. "Mint, you don't sit there."

I blinked. "I don't?"

"No. Your seat is over here." He pointed to the very front row.

Oh.

OH.

I gritted my teeth and shuffled to my assigned seat of shame.

The kids behind me snickered. I resisted the urge to throw lightning at them—until I remembered.

I HAVE NO POWERS.

Uggghhhh....Horrible.

Failure #2: The Pop Quiz Disaster

So apparently, mortals have to answer questions to prove they're not idiots.

The teacher handed me a math quiz.

I stared at it.

I blinked.

I flipped it over.

There were numbers everywhere.

"What in Hades' name is this?" I muttered.

Carlos whispered from beside me. "Dude, it's algebra. Just do it like before."

"Before?"

"You were good at this before your accident."

I snorted.

Yeah, right. I'm a god of lightning and mischief. I do chaos and destruction. Not whatever 'X' is supposed to equal.

I picked up my pencil, wrote "MATH IS FAKE" in the answer box, and turned it in.

Failure #3: The Cafeteria War

By lunchtime, I was ready to bolt.

Carlos led me to the lunch line, where I was greeted by the most terrifying sight of all.

The food.

A gray, lumpy substance plopped onto my tray like it was sent straight from Tartarus.

"What is this?" I whispered.

Carlos looked at me like I was nuts. "Dude. It's mashed potatoes."

"LIES."

There was no way this was safe for human consumption.

I poked it with my fork. It jiggled.

Oh yeah. This was an assassination attempt.

I took my tray and walked to the trash can.

Carlos grabbed my arm. "Wait—dude, don't throw it away! That's the best thing they have!"

I stared at him.

…Was this how mortals lived?

I needed to get back to Olympus. Immediately.

By the end of the day, I had learned three important lessons about human school.

Mortals care too much about numbers.

Their food is probably cursed.

If I don't escape soon, I'm gonna lose my mind.

The gods thought this was a punishment?

Oh no.

This was war.

Chapter 6

"Operation Escape, Attempt #1"

Okay, enough is enough.

I have been stranded in the mortal world for way too long.

I have survived their awful food.

I have endured their ridiculous rules.

I have suffered through this thing they call "homework."

And now?

Now, it's time to LEAVE.

I didn't have my full godly power anymore, but I still had a plan.

I just needed:

A storm big enough to break reality.

Something conductive to channel my lightning.

A high place to stand dramatically while calling upon the heavens.

Lucky for me, I had access to all three.

The storm was easy.

I spent all day in class whispering insults to the sky.

"Hey, clouds, you call that a storm? My grandma can thunder louder than that."

"Oh wow, look at that drizzle. So scary. If only I had an umbrella. Oh wait, I DON'T NEED ONE BECAUSE THIS STORM IS WEAK."

By lunchtime, the sky was furious.

Dark clouds rolled in. Thunder rumbled in the distance. A perfect storm was coming.

Step 1: Complete.

Step 2: Find Something Conductive.

Now, I knew metal worked, but where was I supposed to get a divine lightning rod in middle school?

Then I saw it.

The perfect tool.

A giant, shiny flagpole in the middle of the school yard.

It was tall. It was metal. It was literally sticking out of the ground, begging to be used.

Step 2: Also complete.

Step 3: Find a High Place.

This part was a little tricky.

See, apparently, humans get very nervous when you try to climb on top of buildings.

The janitor yelled at me when I tried to sneak onto the roof.

A teacher stopped me from scaling the football bleachers.

So I did the next best thing.

I climbed onto the bleachers that sit to the right of the pole.

"MINT, WHAT ARE YOU DOING?!" Carlos yelled from below.

"Returning to my rightful place." I gloated.

Carlos looked horrified. So did the other students.

I ignored them. I turned to the flagpole, raised my arms to the storm, and yelled...

"OH, GREAT SKY! HEED MY CALL!"

The yard fell silent. All eyes were on me. This was it. This was my moment.

I slammed my palm onto the flagpole and summoned the lightning.

Or... I tried to. Instead, I got a tiny static shock. Like, the kind you get when you rub your socks on carpet. Yelping, I jerked my hand away.

The sky above did nothing. No blinding bolt of divine energy. No portal ripping through reality. Just some light rain and disappointed thunder.

I froze.

The entire cafeteria just stared.

Some kid coughed.

Someone else laughed.

Then?

EVERYONE LAUGHED.

Carlos buried his face in his hands.

"Bro... what was that?"

I scowled.

"It was supposed to be a dramatic escape."

Carlos wiped a tear from his eye.

"Dude. It looked like you just licked a battery."

The laughter grew louder. I felt my face burn.

This... THIS WAS NOT HOW GODLY ESCAPES WERE SUPPOSED TO GO.

I crossed my arms.

"Fine. Enjoy your jokes. But when I actually leave this pathetic world, you'll all regret doubting me."

A kid from across the yard called, "Okay, Sparky, we'll believe it when we see it!"

Sparky?!

I was going to smite someone.

The janitor grabbed me by my shoulder and drug me down from the bleachers.

"That's enough of that," he muttered. "Principal's office. Now."

I groaned.

Not only did my escape plan fail miserably, but now I was getting punished for it.

At this rate, I'd be stuck in the mortal world forever.

Zeus, I swear, I will have my revenge.

Chapter 7

"It Didn't Work, and Now There's a Fire"

Today is off to an amazing start. I tried to summon a storm portal and failed. Miserably.

I became a school-wide joke.

And now, I'm being dragged to the principal's office by a janitor who looks like he could bench press a minotaur.

Things are not going well.

Carlos tried to catch up as the janitor hauled me down the hall.

"Dude," he hissed, "what were you thinking?!"

"I was thinking," I grumbled, "that I should NOT BE HERE RIGHT NOW."

Carlos sighed. "Well, congrats. Now you're definitely here. Probably in detention, too."

I frowned. "So? Detention is just sitting in a room, right?"

"Uh, yeah. After you get a lecture from the principal."

Oh.

Oh no.

The janitor shoved open a door and dumped me into a very boring office.

There were no flaming torches. No floating orbs of judgment. No throne of skulls.

Just a desk, a bookshelf, and a tired-looking man in a cheap suit.

He folded his hands.

"Mint Johnson."

I crossed my arms.

"I reject that name."

The janitor groaned and left.

The principal sighed.

"Fine. Mint. Do you know why you're here?"

"Because I attempted to call upon the power of the heavens to break reality and return to my rightful place among the gods?" I pouted.

The principal stared at me. I stared back. Then he rubbed his temples.

"Or maybe because you climbed on the bleachers, made a scene, and disrupted your lunch period?"

"Ah. Yes. That too."

Then the fire alarm went off.

BWAAAH! BWAAAH! BWAAAH!

I jumped.

The principal snapped up.

"What the..."

A teacher burst into the room, panting.

"Sir! There's...there's a small fire in the yard near the cafeteria!"

I perked up.

A fire? That was interesting. The principal's gaze slowly shifted back to me and I held up my hands.

"Whoa, whoa, whoa. You think I did this? How? I have been in this room for at least four minutes."

The principal narrowed his eyes.

"Did your... 'lightning stunt' have anything to do with this?"

I opened my mouth.

Then closed it.

Then opened it again.

"Define 'anything to do with this.'"

Five minutes later, I'm standing outside with the rest of the school, watching as the cafeteria ladies panic while putting out small fires across a few of the waste bins near one of the lunch tables.

Carlos elbowed me.

"Dude. What did you do?"

"I don't know!" I whispered. "I didn't even summon lightning!"

"Then how did..."

And that's when I saw it.

A smoking metal fork lying near the flames, between the pole and the metal trash bin.

Oh.

OH.

I had touched the flagpole.

The flagpole was metal.

It had built up static.

 And apparently, some poor, unlucky soul had grabbed a metal fork, touched the trash bin, and completed the circuit.

Cue: tiny shock. Tiny spark. Tiny fire.

Oops.

The principal walked up right then.

"Mint."

I shoved my hands in my pockets. "Yes?"

"...Do you know anything about this?"

I looked him dead in the eyes.

And said, "Absolutely not."

He didn't believe me.

And that's how I ended up in detention on my first week of school.

Thanks, Zeus.

Chapter 8
"School Lunch Is an Abomination" (Confirmed, Again)

Alright.

I had already experienced one tragic encounter with mortal food.

But apparently, I didn't suffer enough.

Because now?

I was in detention.

And as punishment for my so-called 'disruptive behavior', I had to eat lunch detention food.

Which is somehow worse than regular cafeteria food.

Carlos had escaped unscathed from my failed escape plan, but before he left for the normal lunchroom, he had patted my shoulder like I was going to war.

"Stay strong, bro."

I had rolled my eyes. "It's just food. What's the worst that could—"

And then the cafeteria lady dropped a tray in front of me.

I froze.

Oh no.

OH NO.

Now, I've seen monsters.

I've faced Olympian judgment.

I have stood before the wrath of Zeus himself.

And yet.

THIS. THIS RIGHT HERE.

Was the scariest thing I had ever seen.

The tray held three things:

A mystery meat slab that looked like it had been resurrected from the underworld.

Peas that had no right being that shade of green.

And, worst of all... The Mashed Potatoes.

The same ones from before.

They had returned.

Like an unkillable hydra.

I stared at them.

They stared back.

The cafeteria lady smirked.

"Eat up, sweetie."

And then she walked away.

I was officially trapped.

I glanced at the other kids stuck in lunch detention.

Most of them looked defeated. Some were poking their food like it might attack.

One kid?

Straight-up muttered a prayer before taking a bite.

I needed a plan.

A way out.

A way to avoid whatever unholy magic was happening on this tray.

I could throw it away.

Nope. Not happening. The cafeteria lady was watching me like a vulture.

Maybe I could trade with someone else? Looking around confirmed that all of us had received the same slop and no one was eager to have more added.

Which left only one option... destroy it with a lightning bolt.

But then I again remembered...I was without my divine abilities still...

Sighing, I grabbed my fork and poked at the mashed potatoes. They wiggled into an almost ghoulish smile.

Oh gods.

I was going to die here.

The kid next to me leaned over.

"Hey, new kid. You gonna eat that?"

I turned to him, wide-eyed.

"...You want this?"

He nodded. "Yeah, man. I'll take it."

A miracle.

I shoved the tray at him immediately.

"Take it. Take all of it. My gift to you."

The kid smacked his lips and dug in. All I could do was watch in horror. This was it, the bravest human I had ever met.

Chapter 9

"Leave Me Alone Mortal"

S o.

Detention was a bust.

Lunch was a horror show.

My escape attempt failed spectacularly.

At this point, I was just trying to get through the day without embarrassing myself further.

But of course.

Of course, that's when I gained a follower.

It started right after detention.

I was power-walking through the hallway, trying to get to class, when I felt it.

A presence.

A weird, tingling feeling on the back of my neck.

Like I was being watched.

I turned around.

Nothing.

The hallway was full of students, but no one was obviously staring.

I narrowed my eyes. Huh.

Weird.

Next period, I sat down at my desk.

Carlos leaned over. "Dude. Why does Kevin keep staring at you?"

I blinked. "Who?"

Carlos gestured across the room.

I followed his gaze and...BLAM!

Direct eye contact.

A kid with messy hair, wide eyes, and an unsettling leer. I jumped at the sight, making Carlos chuckle.

"Yeah. That's Kevin. He's been watching you all day."

ALL DAY?!

I shook it off. Maybe it was nothing. Maybe Kevin was just weird. Maybe he was looking at the clock behind me. Or the window. Or the...

"Hey."

Kevin was right next to me. I nearly fell out of my chair.

"Uh. Can I help you?" I said, scooting my chair to gain some distance.

Kevin looked smug.

"I know your secret."

My stomach dropped.

Oh no.

"Secret? I don't have a secret. Haha. What are you talking about? I'm totally normal. Haha. Just a regular, average human person. Haha." I laughed nervously.

Kevin nodded.

"Right."

Then he leaned in.

"You have powers. Don't you?"

I froze.

Oh, Zeus.

Oh, Hades.

Oh, EVERYONE.

I HAVE BEEN FOUND OUT.

I needed to play it cool. To deny everything.

Kevin gasped dramatically, "OH MY GOSH. That reaction just CONFIRMED it!"

I slapped my forehead and Carlos burst out laughing.

Kevin grabbed my arm.

"I knew it! I KNEW IT! I SAW WHAT YOU DID AT LUNCH! You tried to summon lightning, right? You're like a superhero or something, aren't you?"

I yanked my arm back.

"No! I'm not a superhero! That was—"

Kevin gasped again.

"OH WOW. You're trying to keep your identity a SECRET, huh?! Like a Comic Hero, or from one of those Superhuman movies! Like...like...Zeus-Man!"

I choked.

"Zeus-Man?! That's NOT a thing!"

Kevin ignored me.

He clasped his hands together.

"Listen, I can help. I'll be your sidekick!"

Sidekick. My chest twisted for a moment. Back home, no one wanted to stand next to me unless they were lecturing me or waiting for me to mess up. And here was this mortal kid... actually choosing me? I hated how much those words dug into me.

Staring at Kevin's beaming smile, I almost missed Carlos' wheezing laughter.

"I can totally keep a secret," he continued. "I haven't even told anyone about the time I saw Mrs. Thompson's wig fly off in the parking lot. AND THAT WAS HUGE."

I buried my face in my hands.

Why me?

For the rest of the day, Kevin followed me. Through the halls. To my locker. To gym class. He even tried to lift weights, saying, "I gotta start training if I'm gonna be your sidekick."

It was unbearable. And no matter what I said, he wouldn't leave me alone. This was almost worst than detention.

By the time the final bell rang, I bolted for the exit, almost free.

"HEY, PARTNER!"

I whipped around and Kevin was right behind me.

I groaned.

"Kevin. Please."

Kevin winked.

"I'll see you tomorrow. We have work to do, boss."

Then he finger-gunned at me.

And walked away.

Carlos clapped me on the back.

"Congrats, dude."

I sighed. "For what?"

"For getting your first fan."

I scowled at him.

Carlos just grinned.

Chapter 10

"What? No power?"

By this time, I had been stuck in the mortal world for a little while now, and I had one important question.

Where were my godly powers?

I mean, sure, Zeus and the elders stripped me of most of my abilities. But come on. I was still a god.

Right?

Right?!

I needed answers.

Which meant I needed an experiment.

A very scientific, very logical, very well-thought-out experiment to see if I still had ANY powers left.

So naturally...

I did the least scientific thing possible.

I walked into gym class, picked up a dodgeball, and chucked it at full strength.

Results:

The ball soared through the air, missing the target completely, and smashed into the scoreboard.

Which broke instantly. A whole blown right through the center.

...Oops.

Coach Wilson blew his whistle so hard I think his lungs collapsed.

"WHO DID THAT?!"

The entire gym fell silent.

A few kids slowly turned toward me, and I immediately pointed at Kevin.

"HE DID IT."

Kevin gasped. "DUDE, NO I DIDN'T."

Coach squinted at me.

"...Mint. Was that you?"

I put on my best innocent face.

"Me? What? No! That wasn't me! It must've been—uh—" I pointed at the dodgeball.

"Ghosts."

Coach pinched the bridge of his nose. "Mint. Do ghosts play dodgeball?"

"...Maybe?"

Detention. Again.

Alright. So maybe I still had super strength.

But what about lightning?

There was only one way to find out.

Test #2: The Vending Machine Theory.

Kevin followed me after school.

"Alright, boss! What's the plan today?"

I sighed. "Kevin. I don't need a sidekick."

Kevin ignored me.

I stopped in front of the school vending machine.

I turned to Kevin. "Watch and learn."

I rubbed my hands together, took a deep breath, and focused.

Summon the storm. Call the power. Charge the energy.

I slapped my palm onto the vending machine.

BZZZT!

A tiny zap of static electricity sparked from my fingertips.

The vending machine made a sad little beep.

And then...

A single bag of chips fell out.

Kevin exploded.

"DUDE. DUDE. YOU HAVE ELECTRIC POWERS!"

I blinked.

Oh.

Oh snap.

I HAVE MY POWERS.

Kevin immediately started losing his mind.

"BRO. DO YOU KNOW WHAT THIS MEANS? YOU CAN ZAP PEO-PLE. YOU CAN POWER CITIES. YOU CAN—"

"I CAN GET FREE SNACKS!" I yelled.

Kevin froze.

"...That too."

Naturally, I did what any sane person would do in this situation.

I slapped the vending machine again.

BZZZT.

Another tiny shock.

Another bag of chips fell out.

Kevin screamed.

"OH MY GOSH. WE'RE GONNA BE RICH."

Fifteen minutes later, I was standing in front of the vending machine with a pile of snacks at my feet a crowd now formed around us.

Moments later Carlos arrived, took one look at the scene, and sighed.

"Oh no. What did you do now?"

I grinned.

"I figured out my superpower."

Carlos looked at the snacks.

Then at me.

Then at Kevin, who was collecting candy bars like a dragon hoarding gold.

"Committing vending machine fraud?!"

Before I could answer, there was a shout from behind us.

"HEY! WHAT DO YOU THINK YOU'RE DOING?!"

The janitor.

The SAME janitor who had dragged me to the principal's office last time.

His face was red. His arms were crossed.

He was not happy.

I panicked and did the only thing I could think of.

I grabbed a bag of chips...

And THREW IT AT KEVIN.

Kevin yelped, fumbling to catch the bag and almost tripped into the janitor.

Carlos wheeze-laughed from the shifted intersection.

And me?

I took off running.

As I sprinted away, I had one thought.

Hmm...maybe I still had powers.

But maybe I should be a little more careful about how I use them.

...Or not.

We'll see.

Chapter 11
"Accidental Legend Status"

Now, let me be clear.

I did not plan for this to happen. And I most certainly wasn't trying to become famous.

All I wanted was a few free snacks.

But apparently, in the mortal world, that's enough to become a legend.

It started the next morning.

I walked into school, and something felt off.

People were whispering and pointing as I walked through the halls between classes. Staring like I had grown a second head.

Weird right?

Once I passed a group of kids in the hallway and caught bits and pieces of their conversation.

"Did you hear?"

"Yeah! It happened near the vending machine!"

"I heard he used magic!"

"No way. It was some kind of high-tech gadget!"

"No, no! Someone told me he's an actual wizard."

I slowed down. What?

Then one of the kids spotted me and his eyes bugged like he'd seen a ghost.

"Oh my gods."

He grabbed his friend.

"It's him! It's the Lightning Phantom!"

...The WHAT?

I blinked.

"The who now?"

Before I could get answers, Kevin appeared out of nowhere.

He threw an arm around me.

"Ah yes. The Lightning Phantom himself."

I groaned.

"Kevin. What did you do?"

Kevin grinned.

"Oh, nothing. Just... might've mentioned to a few people about your amazing, mysterious powers."

I grabbed his shirt.

"HOW MANY PEOPLE, KEVIN?!"

Kevin shrugged.

"Like... the entire school?"

I had no choice but to release him, my hands running through my hair in frustration. Heck, I debated trying to summon a storm just to smite him.

Carlos walked up, laughing.

"Dude, you're basically a superhero now."

"No," I muttered, "I'm a victim of misinformation."

Carlos smirked.

"Too late. You've got a reputation now."

I groaned. This was a certified disaster.

For the rest of the day, people kept staring at me.

Some kids asked me weird questions.

Some were too scared to talk to me at all.

By lunchtime, I had overheard at least five different versions of the vending machine story:

I had zapped it open like a god.

I had hacked it using my mystical energy.

I had bargained with the vending machine spirit to release its bounty.

I was an alien.

I was a lost prince from an electric kingdom.

(That last one was kind of cool, honestly.)

At lunch, I sat down at my usual table.

Kevin plopped down across from me.

Carlos sighed.

"Bro, the rumors are getting worse."

I rubbed my face.

"Tell me about it."

Kevin grinned.

"Oh, don't worry, boss. I've been helping."

Carlos and I stared.

"...Helping?" I repeated.

Kevin nodded.

"I might've added a few details to keep the legend going."

I leaned forward.

"What. Details."

Kevin beamed.

"Oh, just stuff like—how you saved me from a car crash."

"...I WHAT?"

"And how you shut down a school bully with your electric aura."

"KEVIN."

"And how you may or may not have escaped from a top-secret lab."

I slammed my head onto the table.

Carlos burst into laughter.

Kevin patted my shoulder.

"Relax, boss. This is great PR."

It got worse after lunch.

Some kid from the football team walked up to me arms.

"So. I heard you've got like powers and stuff."

I froze.

Seriously! I needed to shut this down and fast.

I smiled.

"Haha. Nope. No powers. Totally normal dude here."

The guy narrowed his eyes.

Then he held out a water bottle.

"Prove it. Charge this."

...Excuse me?

I blinked.

"You want me to...charge your drink?"

He nodded. "Yeah. I need an energy boost for practice."

I stared at him, then made the mistake of glancing at Kevin, who gave me a thumbs-up.

But the slack-jawed expression on Carlo's face could only have been towards the stupidity of the actual request.

I sighed.

"Alright. Fine. I'll do it."

If it would shut him up, why not?

I rubbed my hands together, focusing.

Besides, if this village idiot wanted me to electrify a liquid for him to drink...who was I to deny him? And if it didn't work, at least these rumors would stop spreading.

Inside, I reached for what little ears energy I still felt and touched the bottle.

BZZT.

A tiny static spark zapped the cap, but the bottle didn't change.

The guy frowned.

"Uh...That's it?"

I clapped my hands together.

"Yep! Fully charged! 100% lightning-infused goodness. Enjoy."

The guy just shrugged, popped the cap, and drained half the bottle.

For a second, nothing happened.

Then his hair stood up.

Every strand straight as a pole. It looked like he had just licked a live power line.

Everyone who had stopped to watch lost their mind.

"OH MY GODS, IT WORKED!"

"THE LEGEND IS REAL!"

"HE'S ACTUALLY ELECTRIFIED!"

The guy dropped the bottle.

"DUDE. WHAT DID YOU DO?!"

Watching me panic, Carlos died laughing.

Kevin immediately hyped up the crowd.

"BEHOLD, THE LIGHTNING PHANTOM!"

Before I could react, the school security guard showed up.

"ALRIGHT, THAT'S ENOUGH. MINT, PRINCIPAL'S OFFICE. NOW."

I groaned.

"Again?!"

As I got dragged away, Kevin called out:

"DON'T WORRY, BOSS! YOUR LEGACY LIVES ON!"

I was going to zap him the first chance I got.

Chapter 12

"Prank War with a Mortal"

At this point, I had three certainties in life:

- I was never going to get back home at this rate.

- Kevin was the worst hype man of all time.

- Someone was about to challenge my legendary status.

- And I was right.

I just thought it was going to be hallway drama and cafeteria laughs. I didn't realize this was the moment the whole school, and something way above it, started paying closer attention to me.

After escaping servitude in the depths of detention, I was determined to keep my head down for the rest of the day.

No more stunts.

No more rumors.

And no more getting dragged to the principal's office.

It was time to be normal...at least for the next twenty-four hours.

But of course, the universe had other plans.

The moment I stepped into the hallway, a kid stepped in front of me, smirking. Tall and bulky, he radiated pure smug energy.

I narrowed my eyes.

"Who are you?"

Widening his stance, he crossed his arms.

"The name's Derek."

I had never met him before in my life.

But I already didn't like him.

Kevin appeared out of nowhere.

"Derek!" he gasped. "You dare stand before the Lightning Phantom?"

Derek rolled his eyes.

"Oh, please. I've heard the stories. Not impressed."

"How dare you?" Kevin gasped. Clutching his chest, he fell back into Carlos, who pushed him quickly into the nearby locker.

I tucked my thumbs into the pockets of my jeans.

"Alright, Derek. What's your problem?"

Derek smirked.

"I just think it's funny. One little trick with a vending machine and suddenly, you're some kind of legend?"

I could do nothing but frown.

"Hey, I didn't start the rumors."

Kevin chimed in.

"I did, your Phantom-ness! You're welcome!"

Derek ignored him, singling me out with a pointed finger.

"I'm calling you out, Sparky."

I blinked.

"...Calling me out?... Sparky!?"

"That's right."

Derek's grin widened as he leaned in.

"Prank Duel."

The hallway erupted.

Kids gasped.

A few whispered, "Oh snap."

And Kevin immediately lost his mind.

"THE CHALLENGER HAS APPEARED!" he yelled. "DO YOU ACCEPT, O GREAT LIGHTNING PHANTOM?"

I rubbed my face.

Why did I have to deal with this?

Derek smirked.

"So? What do you say, Johnson? You up for it?"

Exhaling deeply, I closed my eyes.

Did I want to get involved in this? No.

Was my godly pride going to let me back down? Also no.

I grinned.

"Oh, it's on, mortal."

THE RULES OF PRANK DUEL:

No snitching.

No serious harm.

The first one to give up or get caught loses.

Winner? Crowned ultimate prankster champion.

Kevin insisted on writing the rules down on an actual scroll.

Carlos insisted we were all idiots.

Derek launched the opening salvo.

The next morning, I walked to my locker and opened it.

Instantly...FOOM!

A flour bomb exploded in my face, the entire hallway bursting into laughter. As I stood there, blinking through a cloud of white dust, Derek strolled past, finger guns blasting.

"Stay sharp, Sparky!"

See.... I had thought he would be more elegant in his trickery. After that initial declaration, I assumed a date would be provided. But no, this mortal had dared dispense with the natural pleasantries of godly prank warfare.

He wanted a war?

Fine, I, Mintavious Olemar Johaneson. The God of Lightning and Mischief, the god who had warred with the great Loki since his birth, would be his opponent. And I...I don't lose!

My retaliation was swift and just. For once Kevin was of use to me. He discovered that Derek was picky about which milk carton he would obtain daily. Borrowing some red food dye and vinegar from the science lab, I snuck into the cafeteria.

Derek's usual milk carton?

Now bright pink and...tart.

At lunch, I watched from a distance as Derek picked up his milk, took a sip—and instantly spit it out.

Derek wiped his mouth, scowling.

His gaze met mine and I smirked, giving a quick nod.

"Touché Sparky. Touché."

About a week later, Derek swapped out my gym shoes with ones a size too small. Since Coach Wilson 'requires' us to wear these special shoes, I spent an entire PE period waddling like a penguin.

At one point Kevin joined me in my waddling.

"Boss, are you okay?"

All I could do was watch my subordinate waddle beside me with a comfort I'd not yet felt around him.

"I AM SUFFERING."

Of course I couldn't let that pass. So once my feet stopped throbbing a few days later, I attacked. Rigging Derek's fourth-period chair to make a loud whoopee cushion sound every time he sat, let's just say class was quite amusing. Oh, did I mention, we were in choir, and today was when we were doing a special piece that required us to continuously stand as we sang our round?

Classic? Yes.

Effective? Absolutely.

Even the director laughed.

From there, it escalated.

Derek put glue on my locker handle, so I filled his backpack with packing peanuts.

He put fake spiders in my desk and I messed with his ringtone, making it play a screaming goat in class. That one even made Kevin a little concerned. At recess that day, Kevin sat across from me on the bench.

"Boss, I think this is getting out of hand."

I steepled my fingers, elbows on the table, before responding.

"IT'S ABOUT HONOR NOW."

Then Derek made a big mistake.

He went for THE PRANK TO END ALL PRANKS.

The next morning, everywhere...and I mean everywhere...was my face.

Printed-out pictures of me.

Horrible, mid-sneeze pictures.

Bad school ID photo pictures.

Hand-drawn "Lightning Phantom" artwork.

And not just in the classroom.

ALL. OVER. THE. SCHOOL.

The entire student body was giggling at me. This guy even placed Kevin in a state of awe.

Carlos shook his head.

"I can't even be mad. This is art."

Derek leaned against the lockers, smirking.

"Checkmate."

I stared.

I breathed.

I nodded.

"Well played."

The hallway roared around us, paper versions of my stupid mortal face flapping on every surface. For a second, it felt almost like Olympus again; crowds, spectacle, everyone watching what I'd do next. And under all the noise, that same prickling sensation from the fall brushed the back of my neck, like an invisible eye blinking awake.

This wasn't just a prank war anymore.

This was a signal flare.

Chapter 13

"The School Principal Might Be My New Nemesis"

Let's tally my recent life disasters:

I have been sentenced to live as a mortal.

I have been to detention twice already.

I have somehow gained a sidekick.

I have accidentally become a school legend.

And now?

I had just declared war on a human named Derek.

And it was going great!

Right up until I got summoned to the principal's office.

Kevin patted my back as I got up from my desk.

"Don't worry, boss. If you don't come back, I'll tell your story."

Carlos chuckled.

"Yeah. We'll even make a statue in your honor."

I glared.

"If I don't come back, it's because the principal threw me into Tartarus."

Kevin gasped.

"Wait. Is that a real place?"

I ignored him and marched out the door.

The walk to the principal's office felt longer than usual.

I got a few concerned looks.

One teacher muttered, "Not again."

Some kid saluted me.

(Which was weird, but I'll allow it.)

By the time I reached the office, I was mentally prepared for the worst. Before I could knock, the door swung open, and there he was.

Principal Warren.

Now, let me explain something about Principal Warren.

I have been in front of gods.

I have stood before Zeus himself.

I have survived cosmic judgment.

And yet, this man's glare?

It made me sweat.

He gestured for me to sit, and not wanting to dig any deeper into whatever hole I was currently in, followed the order.

He leaned forward and folded his hands.

"Mint."

I cleared my throat. "Yes?"

"Do you know why you're here?"

I smiled innocently.

"Because I'm a great student and you wanted to personally congratulate me?"

The stare intensified.

"No."

He sighed, then pulled out a stack of papers.

"Let's go over some things, shall we?"

He flipped to page one.

"Four Weeks ago: Lightning stunt in the cafeteria."

I scratched my head. "Okay, in my defense, that was an accident."

He flipped to the next page.

"Three Weeks ago: Mysterious pink milk incident."

"...Allegedly."

Flip.

"Two Weeks ago: Gym shoe sabotage."

"Okay, technically, I was the victim."

Flip.

"Last Week: Screaming goat ringtone in class."

"...That was funny."

He did not laugh.

Flip.

"And today? Hundreds of your face are plastered all over the school."

He paused on that line, tapping the folder with one finger.

"And that's just the stuff I can write down," he muttered. "Fire alarms, blown fuses, weird power surges every time you're in a room ... the district thinks it's a wiring problem."

His eyes lifted to mine.

"I don't."

I sat in silence.

Then I slowly leaned forward.

"So... what's my score?"

Principal Warren closed the folder before leaning back in his chair.

"Mint."

"Yes?"

"I need you to understand something."

He took a deep breath.

Then, in a very calm, very serious voice, he said:

"I am tired."

I blinked.

"...Tired?"

"Yes. Tired. Exhausted. Drained. Because of YOU."

I pointed at myself.

"Me? I barely do anything."

"BARELY?!"

He slapped the folder.

"Mint, you have been back here for one month. One. Month. And some-how, you have gone from one of our school's star pupils to my greatest challenge."

I gasped.

"Wow. That's actually a huge honor."

The joke popped out on instinct, but it didn't land right in my own chest.

Back on Olympus, being "a problem" made me feel powerful.

Here, it just made me look ... broken.

"It's NOT."

He rubbed his temples.

"Listen. I don't know why this change occurred in you. I don't know what planet you think you're from. But I do know this; if I see you in here again, I will make your life a living nightmare."

I perked up.

"Oh. Been there, done that."

His hands stopped circling his temples, and I cleared my throat.

"Uh. I mean. Duly noted."

He stood up.

"Now. I am giving you one more chance."

I nodded seriously.

"Yes, sir."

"You will leave this office and return to class."

"Yes, sir."

"And you will not pull any more pranks."

"Absolutely, sir."

"And you will not get involved in any more chaos."

"Of course, sir."

"Good."

He narrowed his eyes.

"...And just to be sure, I will be watching you. Very closely."

I walked out of the office without another word.

The moment I stepped into the hallway, Kevin and Carlos were waiting.

Kevin grinned. "Well..."

Carlos finished where he left off, "...Did you get expelled?"

I shrugged past them, heading back to class.

"No."

Kevin cheered.

"YES! We live to prank another day!"

I held up a hand. "Whoa, whoa, whoa. No. No more pranks."

They both froze.

Carlos raised an eyebrow.

"Wait. What?"

I lowered my voice.

"The principal is onto me. I have to lay low for a while."

Kevin gasped.

"Boss. You're going undercover?"

"...Sure. Let's call it that."

Carlos rolled his eyes.

"Well this is going to end badly."

All I could think was, Yeah. Probably.

Chapter 14
"Operation Escape, Attempt #2"

Despite the 'strong' warning, I was not about to lay low. Let's face it, there was no way I was staying stuck in the mortal world forever. I had a reputation to rebuild. A divine reputation. Which meant there was no way I was letting Derek continue to prank me while I was under surveillance. I needed an exit strategy. Not just for the mortal world, but to get out of school for the rest of the day, and it had to be sneaky.

Lightning portal? ...had not worked.

Summoning my godly power? Also had not worked.

Hiding from Kevin? ... also not working.

So it was time to try something new.

This time, I wasn't going to rely on powers.

This time, I was going full stealth mode.

The first step was to find a proper exit. Now, obviously, just walking out of school wasn't an option.

Principal Warren had his beady little eyes on me at all times. So I needed a different route. That's when I remembered the janitor's closet. See, the janitor's closet wasn't just a closet. It had a maintenance tunnel, and that tunnel led outside.

It was the perfect escape route.

Step two: Acquire a distraction.

That's where Kevin came in.

"Alright, boss," he said. "What's the plan?"

I folded my arms.

"I need you to cause chaos."

Kevin beamed.

"Say no more."

Five minutes later, a fire alarm went off.

I don't know what Kevin did, and honestly? I didn't want to know.

All that mattered was that the entire school was freaking out.

Students poured into the hallways. Teachers yelled. Some kid dropped a whole tray of nachos.

It was beautiful.

I slipped away undetected.

Ducked into the janitor's closet.

Pulled open the tunnel door.

And just like that, I was one step closer to Olympus.

It was dark in the tunnel.

Dusty. Creepy. Probably filled with rats.

(Or worse, high school memories left behind by previous students.)

But none of that mattered; I was about to be free.

Halfway down, the hairs on my arms stood up. The overhead bulbs flickered a few times, almost as if some being was squinting at me through the concrete. It was the same crawling feeling from my fall out of Olympus, that invisible spotlight sliding over my skin.

Only this time, I wasn't plummeting through clouds.

I was in a mortal school basement, and whatever was watching felt closer.

Then I hit a dead end.

Literally.

Because guess who was standing at the exit?

Principal Warren.

I froze as he pulled out a ring of keys and looked toward the door behind him.

There was a long, painful silence.

Then, in the most tired voice I have ever heard in my immortal existence, he said:

"...Really?"

I considered my options.

Try to outrun him. (Unlikely. The man had weirdly fast reflexes.)

Pretend I was sleepwalking. (Would've been convincing if I hadn't literally just run down here.)

Play dead. (A solid strategy... but probably not the best one.)

Instead, I went with Option 4.

I grinned.

"Oh, hey, Principal Warren! Fancy meeting you here! What brings you down to this totally normal maintenance tunnel?"

His eye twitched.

"Mint."

"Yes?"

He took a deep breath.

"This is your third escape attempt."

I gasped. "Third? No way. This is only my... wait." I counted on my fingers. "Oh. Yeah, no, you're right. Third."

His jaw clenched.

"This is getting ridiculous."

I threw my hands up. "Okay, but is it really my fault? I mean, I don't belong here. This whole mortal school thing just isn't working out for me."

He pinched the bridge of his nose.

"Mint. You are a student here. You do belong here."

I snorted.

"Hah. No. That's the thing, sir. I don't."

He lowered his voice.

"You're right."

I blinked.

"...Wait, what?"

"You don't belong here."

He folded his arms.

"You're smart, Mint. I can see that. And you are different from the other students. I don't know how, exactly. But what I do know?"

He leaned forward.

"You have a choice."

That actually threw me off.

I expected anger.

I expected detention.

I expected getting dragged back to class.

But this?

This was worse.

Because Principal Warren wasn't mad.

He was disappointed.

"If you want to waste your time pulling stunts like this," he said, "that's your decision."

I opened my mouth to argue.

But he wasn't done.

"But if you're looking for a way out? If you really want to prove you're better than all of this?"

He crossed his arms.

"Then stop running. And start actually doing something."

I didn't know how to respond to that.

So I just stood there.

For the first time since arriving in the mortal world... I had no comeback.

And that?

That was deeply unsettling.

Between his glare, the flickering light, and that invisible pressure pressing down from somewhere above the ceiling, it hit me:

I wasn't just dodging principals and pranks anymore.

Every stunt I pulled was sending a signal.

If I kept running in circles down here, something else was going to answer before Zeus ever did.

"Think about it," he said, turning away.

And just like that, he walked back up the tunnel.

Leaving me standing in the dark.

I stayed there for a while.

Processing.

Annoyed.

Maybe a little...confused.

But mostly?

I just didn't like that he had a point.

I dragged myself back to class.

Kevin gasped when he saw me.

"Boss! You're alive!"

Carlos raised an eyebrow. "Wait, did you...actually come back on your own?"

I flopped into my chair.

Kevin and Carlos stared at me.

"...Mint?"

I scowled.

"Shut up. I'm thinking... if I can't get out, maybe I can drag a little of Olympus down here instead."

Chapter 15

"Oops, I Summoned a Monster"

Alright.

I have got to be losing my edge. Not even Loki had pulled off what Principal Warren had just done. A very concerning development. But that's ok. If I couldn't escape on my own, I just needed to call for help.

Someone from the celestial world. Someone who could bust me out.

A god. A titan. A mythical ally.

A totally reliable divine backup plan.

So naturally, I ended up summoning a monster instead.

It wasn't supposed to go wrong.

I had the plan. I had the incantation. I even had the chalk and candles, which I'm pretty sure are required for this sort of thing.

Kevin, unfortunately, insisted on being there.

He sat cross-legged on the floor, watching me draw symbols.

"So let me get this straight," he said. "You're actually magic?"

I rolled my eyes. "Kevin, I have been struck by lightning multiple times and I'm still alive. What do you think?"

Kevin gasped. "So that's why your hair is so cool."

I ignored him.

Carlos stood by the door, leaning against the frame.

"This is a terrible idea."

I waved him off.

"That's your opinion."

Kevin tilted his head.

"Wait, what's the goal again?"

I grinned.

"Summon a messenger from Olympus. Get them to deliver me to some distant cloud until the gods finally calm down, and Boom... instant get-out-of-mortal-jail-free card!"

Carlos groaned.

"You're literally about to summon an ancient, godly being in a middle school bathroom."

"Yeah?"

"Yeah, no, that's peak bad decision-making."

I clapped my hands.

"Alright! Here we go!"Kevin cheered.

Focusing, I sketched the needed magical circle, chanting the incantation as I went; power flowing into each runic inscription as it was finished. When the chalk and wax finally met to complete the circle, a faint spark of golden light flickered through the air. Whether that caused the next events... well, I'm just going to assume they did.

The room buzzed. The air crackled. And in the center of the circle, a shimmering ring began to appear. Something dark seeped into the ring of light, and I held my breath.

Kevin's eyes widened despite the steady stream of chips being pumped into his mouth. Carlos placed one foot outside the door, using the wall to block the majority of his vital organs.

And then—

BOOM.

The floor shook. The lights flickered. The bathroom stall doors slammed open.

And instead of a helpful godly messenger...

A gigantic, glowing, vaguely wolf-shaped beast with too many eyes and entirely too many teeth emerged from the summoning circle, snarling.

Kevin screamed, chips flying as he flailed.

Carlos held his breath, sliding further behind the wall.

"Oh crap. That's not Hermes." I said, scrambling backwards like a crab.

The monster locked eyes with me.

Well, some of them did; the rest seemed to be analyzing its current situation.

Then it lunged.

Dodging under a stall door, it barely missed me. Kevin tried to climb onto the sink, while carlos darted to the other side of the door frame to keep it from slamming shut on us.

"YO! MOVE! COME ON!"

We burst into the hallway, tearing down the science wing like trackstars. We didn't look back, didn't need to; because two seconds later the crumbling sound of brick was followed by the screams of students and teachers alike.

The beast, having crashed through the doorway, snarled and knocked over everything in sight.

And that's when I realized—

I had just unleashed a divine beast into the school.

On Olympus, breaking stuff was ... expected. Pillars regrow. Gods respawn. Immortals can tank a lot of bad decisions.

Here, the screams sounded different.

Human.

Fragile.

One swipe from that thing and it wouldn't be a funny story or a lecture from Zeus, it would be a disaster I couldn't charm my way out of.

"MINT!" Carlos shoved me. "FIX IT!"

"I'M THINKING!"

Kevin sprinted next to us.

"What is that thing?!"

I racked my brain.

"Uh. Maybe an underworld beast? A lesser chaos entity? An escaped cosmic guard dog?"

"CAN YOU CONTROL IT?"

"Absolutely not."

The monster snarled and charged down the hall.

Lockers crashed open. Books went flying.

I had seconds before this turned into a full disaster.

I needed to banish it.

Skidding to a stop, I let Kevin and Carlos pass me, turning to face the monster alone. Bracing my wrist I called for all the lingering power I had at my disposal.

Lightning crackled. Power rippled through me.

I focused on the exact words I needed.

A command. A banishing phrase.

I took a deep breath.

And shouted:

"HEY, BAD DOG! GO BACK TO YOUR DIMENSION!"

There was a long pause.

Carlos who had stopped once they noticed I was no longer with them, groaned. "That's your spell?"

The monster blinked, almost confused. Then it let out a distorted, grumbling growl. And just like that—POOF.

It vanished.

Kevin cheered.

"YOU DID IT!"

I exhaled, wiping my forehead. "Well, that was easy."

Then the fire alarm went off and Carlos grabbed me by the arm.

"Run."

I didn't argue.

We sprinted out of the hallway, and behind us, students were losing their minds.

Some kid yelled, "IT WAS A DEMON! WE'RE ALL DOOMED!"

Another shouted, "IT WAS THE LIGHTNING PHANTOM! HE SUM-MONED IT!"

Kevin pumped his fist.

"Boss, you're officially the most powerful being in school!"

Carlos corrected him.

"No, he's officially the most screwed being in school."

And then I heard the worst sound possible.

A very familiar, very angry voice.

"MINT JOHNSON!"

I winced. Peaking my head back down the intersecting hall we'd just crossed, I tried my best "It wasn't me this time" smile.

There, standing at the end of the hall, covered in chaos, glaring as if I had personally ruined his entire week, was Principal Warren.

I sighed.

"Yeah, okay. That's fair."

Chapter 16

"Avoiding Doom" (While Doing Homework)

Shall we take a moment to acknowledge the unfairness of the universe? Sure, I may have accidentally summoned a divine beast into the school. And sure, technically, I might have caused a school-wide panic.

And yes, fine, maybe I've spent more time in detention than in actual class. But did I deserve what was coming next?

Ok, probably.

Principal Warren didn't even yell this time, which was worse.

Because you know you've really messed up when someone just stares at you in pure, silent disappointment.

I sat in the principal's office, slouched in the chair.

Kevin was next to me, looking way too pleased about all of this. Carlos stood behind us, arms crossed, shaking his head like a concerned parent. And Principal Warren?

He just exhaled.

"Mint," he said.

"Sup."

He didn't react. Just sat there, rubbing his temples.

Finally, he looked up.

"You summoned a giant, mythical, many-eyed creature into my school."

I nodded.

"Correct."

"I'm not even going to ask how you know how to do that. I'm not even going to ask why. But you caused a school-wide panic."

"Thank you sir, and also...correct."

"You have put me in a position where I now have to explain this mess to the school board."

"Oof. That one's on you."

Kevin snorted and Carlos kicked my chair.

I propped a single elbow on the table and held up my hand.

"Look, I understand that mistakes were made."

Principal Warren narrowed his eyes.

"Mistakes?"

I cleared my throat.

"Okay, several mistakes. Possibly dozens. But in my defense..."

He raised a hand.

"If you say 'this is not entirely my fault,' I will lose my last shred of patience."

I shut my mouth.

I had one brain cell still firing and it told me to shut up immediately.

Principal Warren leaned forward.

"You're officially banned from unsupervised science experiments, rituals, or anything involving candles in this school."

Kevin gasped.

"Wait, so he was doing magic?"

Carlos groaned.

"Kevin, we literally just saw a monster appear out of thin air."

Kevin shrugged.

"Yeah, but I thought maybe it was, like, really advanced technology or something."

My face dropped into my hands.

"Kevin, stop helping."

The principal pointed at me.

"You will serve detention every day this week. And during detention? You will actually do your classwork."

I gasped.

"You mean actual homework?"

"Yes."

"But...but that's cruel and unusual punishment!"

Principal Warren leaned back in his chair, pointing to a bucket and mop in the corner.

"Would you rather clean the cafeteria and bathrooms?"

The thought of what the bathroom must look like after the beast made me shudder.

"I'll take the homework."

And that's how I ended up sitting in an empty classroom after school, doing actual schoolwork for the first time.

Kevin, of course, was still here. Carlos too, had stayed

Apparently, my so-called 'friends' thought this was hilarious.

Kevin leaned over my desk.

"So, boss, what exactly was that thing you summoned?"

I tapped my pencil on my paper.

"Dunno. But it was definitely not an Olympian."

Carlos had been deep in his phone, turning it around to show a spreadsheet document.

"It looked kinda like a guardian beast. You know, the ones that protect divine vaults or temples?"

I raised an eyebrow.

"So you're saying I basically summoned a giant, angry security guard?"

Carlos nodded.

"Pretty much."

I considered that, then smirked.

"Well, I regret nothing."

Kevin just nodded confidently, while Carlos went back to typing notes and rolling a sucker around in his mouth.

The teacher monitoring detention fluffed their newspaper and somewhere in the universe, the gods were definitely facepalming.

Chapter 17

"Fine, I'll Handle the Monster Myself"

I never planned on seeing that monster again. It was supposed to be gone. Banished. Yeeted back into whatever chaos dimension it came from.

So when I woke up the next morning and felt the static charge in the air, I knew something was wrong.

Kevin and Carlos met me at my locker.

Carlos looked annoyed, which is his default expression when I do something dumb.

Kevin, as usual, looked way too excited about the situation.

"So, boss," Kevin said. "Good news or bad news first?"

I closed my locker.

"Neither. Just tell me what happened."

"Fine," Carlos said, pulling out his phone, "The monster isn't gone."

I blinked.

"Excuse me?"

"Yep," Kevin nodded smugly. "It's been spotted around town."

I stared.

"What do you mean, 'spotted around town'?"

Carlos turned his phone towards me as Kevin spun behind me, giddy as a kid in a candy store.

On the screen, a blurry video of a security camera clip from a gas station. At first, nothing happened. The camera was watching the gas pumps from the streetlight. Then, a huge, shadowy creature with glowing eyes and way too many legs skittered across the screen.

The clip cut out immediately after.

Kevin grinned. "Pretty sick, right?"

I shoved the phone back at Carlos.

"It didn't have those extra legs last time, did it?"

"Nope," Carlos said, scrolling through the other videos and taking out a new sucker. "Looks like I was right, it's a Helios Guard and it's evolving."

This new calm of his was starting to unnerve me.

"Okay. So. We have a giant cosmic guard dog loose in the mortal world."

Carlos nodded, and I took a deep breath.

And then, like the mature, responsible god I am—

I immediately tried to leave.

"Where are you going?" Carlos demanded.

"Away."

"You caused this!"

"Yeah, and I fixed it!"

Carlos waved his phone. "Oh yeah? Tell that to the blurry security footage."

Kevin put a hand on my shoulder.

"Boss. It's time to take responsibility."

I stared at him.

"...Kevin, are you okay?"

Kevin nodded solemnly.

"I just think, as a god, it's your duty to protect humanity."

I squinted.

"...Did you just copy that from a superhero movie?"

He winked. "Absolutely. How'd I sound? Cool, right?"

Carlos pocketed his phone.

"Look. I don't care what you do, but if Principal Warren finds out about this, you're done."

That got my attention.

See, I could deal with monsters. I could deal with Kevin being weird.

But I was not dealing with more detention.

That's where I drew the line.

"Fine," I groaned, "I'll 'handle' it."

Kevin cheered.

"YES! Operation 'Mint vs. The Monster' is a go!"

Carlos squinted, his brows in pain from that last comment. Looking at Mint through a single eye he asked, "Do you even have a plan?"

I grinned.

"Obviously."

Carlos waited.

I blinked.

"...Okay, no. But I will in like five minutes."

Carlos sighed.

"We're gonna die."

That night, I set up a trap. Or, well, an 'almost trap.'

Step one:

Find a way to lure the monster out.

Step two:

Contain it.

Step three:

Make it go away.

Simple, right?

Wrong.

Because as soon as the sun went down, I realized I had no clue what I was doing. Kevin had brought snacks. Carlos had brought logic. And I... I had brought absolutely nothing useful.

Kevin crunched annoyingly on some chips.

"Sooo... how exactly do we find it? Do you have some kind of celestial dog whistle?"

Smugly I stuck out my chest.

"Easy. We wait."

Carlos stared.

"We wait? That's it? That's the plan? Stand here... at a "RANDOM" gas station and wait?"

"Yep."

Carlos looked at Kevin.

"Your boss is an idiot. You know that, right?"

Kevin nodded, nudging him with his elbow.

"Yeah, but he's our idiot."

Suddenly, the wind shifted; air crackling with energy.

A slight static charge, a presence.

The beast was here.

I slowly turned away from the bright overhead lights, peering into the darkness, where two glowing eyes stared back at me.

Kevin dropped his chips and Carlos uttered something that sounded like a prayer.

And me?

I did the only logical thing.

I grinned.

"Alright, big guy," I said. "Round two. Let's go."

Chapter 18
"Wait, This Thing Is Actually Scary"

Okay.

So maybe I underestimated the situation.

Like, just a little.

Because staring into the darkness, locking eyes with a giant cosmic beast made of shadows and nightmares, I was starting to think...

Yeah.

This was a terrible idea.

It moved first.

One second, it was across the lot, barely visible in the shadows.

The next?

Right in front of me.

I didn't even see it move. Didn't hear it.

It was just there.

What was worst, I felt it. This deep, low vibration in my chest. Not a growl. Something far worse. A sound that didn't belong in this world.

I tried to summon a spark.

Nothing.

I swallowed.

"Okay, wow. That's unsettling."

Kevin, standing way too close behind me, whispered, "Boss, what's the plan?"

Carlos, from several feet further away (because Carlos is smart) whisper shouted, "Yeah, Mint. What's the plan?"

I slowly took a step back.

"I am currently… assessing my options."

The monster tilted its head and a new set of eyes blinked open on its shoulders.

Okay. Yeah. Nope. That was way too unsettling.

"New plan!" I yelled. "We run!"

Kevin shrieked, "Great plan!" and took off.

Carlos didn't even wait for the command. He was already halfway gone.

That, unfortunately, was about the only thing I saw before.

"THUUUNNNGGG!!"

I ran directly into a dumpster.

The impact knocked the wind out of me, causing me to stumble back, dazed, and blinking stars out of my vision.

As for the monster?

It didn't move.

Didn't charge.

Didn't even flinch.

It just… watched.

Carlos skidded to a stop, realizing I wasn't behind him.

Kevin, from a safe distance, yelled, "Boss, you good?"

I lifted a very wobbly thumbs-up.

"Y-yeah! Totally fine! That was… what you call a strategic move."

Carlos panted. "Bro! You ran into a dumpster."

"Look, mistakes were made…" I huffed.

But before I could finish the beast moved and for the first time all night, it spoke.

"You are not ready."

I froze.

Carlos and Kevin went dead silent.

The voice wasn't a growl.

It wasn't a roar, or a hiss, or a guttural nightmare sound. It was… calm. Smooth. And extremely deep.

Almost like it wasn't talking with a mouth, but directly into my mind.

I hated that.

"…Uh." I took a half-step backward. "Excuse me?"

The monster did not elaborate.

It just continued standing there. Watching.

Then, in the blink of an eye, it turned and vanished.

Gone.

Not some magic trick poof of smoke. Just… not there anymore. Like it was never there to begin with.

Kevin, still hiding behind a mailbox, called out, "Did we win?"

Carlos stared at the empty space where the monster had been mouth wide open in amazement.

I let out a breath I didn't realize I was holding.

"No," I winced, touching the knot on my forehead. "We definitely didn't win."

For the first time since I'd arrived in the mortal world, something didn't just feel wrong.

It felt bigger.

Like I'd set something in motion that wasn't going to stop.

Not for me.

Not for Kevin, still hiding behind mailboxes and dumpsters like that would actually save him.

Not for Carlos, who pretended he didn't care but had still come running back when he thought I might be monster food.

And realizing they were on the board now too?

That was terrifying.

But obviously, I wasn't about to admit any of those feelings.

Dusting myself off, I squared my shoulders, and grinned.

"Well," I said. "I regret nothing."

But I just couldn't shake the very bad feeling that had sunk into my bones.

Chapter 19

"Operation Escape, Attempt #3" (For Real This Time)

This time, it had to work. There was no way I was staying on this dumb mortal rock any longer. Not even trying to conjure a godly favor had succeeded. Everything had failed spectacularly.

But this next plan was foolproof.

Carlos stared at my setup.

"...This is your plan?"

Kevin nodded approvingly.

"I like it."

"That's how I know it's a bad idea," Carlos said, shaking his head.

I spread my arms, proudly presenting my latest stroke of genius.

The plan was simple. Ride the monster's divine energy straight back to Olympus. If it could enter this world, that meant it could leave. And if it could leave... I could hitch a ride.

This wasn't like the janitor tunnel or a lightning-portal fail. If this worked, I'd be back in the clouds. If it didn't ... then I'd just flashed a giant "Here I Am" sign across every plane that had noticed me falling out of Olympus.

Carlos crossed his arms.

"Mint. You don't even know where it came from."

"That's the fun part! It's a mystery!"

"Do you at least know how to control it?"

"...Define 'control.'"

Carlos dragged a hand down his face.

Kevin, meanwhile, was eating popcorn.

Because of course he was.

"So, boss. How do we summon the beast?"

I smirked.

"Easy."

And then, before Carlos could protest—

I threw a lightning bolt into the sky.

The bolt snapped through the clouds, a brilliant beacon shooting skyward; then nothing.

Just a silent night, with Kevin munching away, Carlos' face still residing in his palm, and me, arms akimbo, grinning like the absolute genius I am.

Then, one low, distant rumble that didn't sound like any storm I'd ever heard. The hairs on my arms rose, that invisible spotlight from my fall sliding over me again. Only this time it hit me like a hammer.

And from the darkness...

It came.

The monster emerged from the shadows, its many eyes glowing.

Carlos immediately took three steps back. But what did Kevin do? Pull out his phone.

"Ohhh, sick."

I stood my ground.

"Alright, big guy," I said, rolling my shoulders. "We're gonna make a deal."

The beast tilted its head.

Carlos, still backpedaling, whispered, "Mint. This is a terrible—"

"I offer you a trade."

No fear. No hesitation. I was in control.

The monster blinked, taking a step closer.

I kept my voice even.

"I need to get back to Olympus."

It didn't move.

"And I think," I continued, "you can help me do that."

Now you know that moment where you aren't sure if your bluff worked...yeah...

Then, finally—

It spoke.

"You misunderstand."

My smirk faltered.

"...Uh. Sorry, what?"

The air around us crackled.

The monster wasn't just watching me now.

It was studying me.

Carlos hissed, "Mint, I really don't think—"

But the monster wasn't listening to him. Its voice rumbled directly into my mind.

"I do not serve the gods."

"I do not follow your will."

"I was sent for you."

I blinked.

"Wait...Wait...Come again?"

The monster's many eyes burned into me.

"You are being watched, Thunderbrat."

"Forces beyond Olympus take interest in you."

"And they are waiting."

The wind whipped around me, charged with energies I had never encountered.

For the first time in my immortal life...

I didn't know what to say.

Then, as suddenly as it arrived...the monster vanished. A slight misty trail dissipating in it's wake.

Carlos exhaled, spitting the remnants of his sucker stick into a nearby garbage can.

"Okay. That was horrifying."

Kevin, still nervously munching on popcorn, nodded.

"Yeah, boss. I don't think that thing's your pet."

I didn't answer.

Because suddenly, I had a much, much bigger problem than Zeus.

Every stunt I'd pulled to get out, every bolt, every circle, every "oops" in the mortal world, had been lighting me up on something else's radar.

This wasn't just about escaping anymore.

It was about surviving whoever was watching.

Chapter 20

"Back to Olympus?"

I was not okay.

Like, at all.

See, when you make a brilliant escape plan, it usually goes one of two ways:

It works. (This has never happened to me.)

It explodes in my face. (This happens constantly.)

But this?

This was worse.

Because the monster wasn't just watching me.

It was waiting.

Kevin nudged me as we walked back towards the school.

"Sooo, boss... does that mean we win?"

Carlos groaned. "Kevin. No one is winning."

I barely heard them.

Because my brain was too busy screaming.

Who was watching me?

Why was this thing sent for me?

And—more importantly—Who sent it and what did it want?

And that's when it returned.

One second, there was nothing.

The next—

A wall of static-charged darkness filled the air.

The monster didn't step out of the shadows.

It was the shadows.

Surging forward, the darkness curled around me. There were no words, not attack, just the pressure of being grabbed by an invisible giant.

Now.

I'm an immortal god.

A child of Olympus.

I have divine lightning at my command. (Well, had...)

I should be impossible to move against my will.

But guess what?

This thing didn't care.

The second its shadowy limbs coiled around me, the world twisted sideways and everything went white.

Words wouldn't form, thoughts scattered, and my eyes drifted from your average street into a medley of galactic starscapes.

I blinked. Then blinked again. The glinting specks of light in the darkness had grown so bright it blinded me. Stung by their shine, my eyes closed hard and when they opened, I was standing on clouds. Floating in the sky. A deep, endless blue stretched in every direction.

And before me?

The gates of Olympus.

For half a second, my chest actually ached. I remembered the crackle of full power running through my veins, lightning on demand, flying above storms instead of face-planting into them. No homework. No principals. No cafeteria food that might legally be classified as a weapon.

In that moment, I wanted it back.

All of it.

I stumbled back.

"No. Nope. Absolutely not."

Because this wasn't just any entrance.

This was the grand entrance.

The main gates of the gods.

The place Zeus himself watches over.

The single worst place I could possibly be.

And I was standing right in front of it.

Kevin's voice echoed in my head.

"Boss. It's your duty to protect humanity."

Ha.

Joke's on him.

I was not protecting anyone right now.

I was about to die.

A deep boom shook the sky, storm clouds now churning above me. I looked around, but the beast was gone.

"Traitor."

From above a massive golden figure appeared with lightning crackling around him. Thunder rumbled with his every breath, and his expression?

Not happy.

Zeus, King of the Gods, and my LEAST favorite parental figure, landed; voice rippling through entirety of the realm.

"You return?"

I cleared my throat, straightened my shoulders, and grinned.

"Sup, Pops?"

Chapter 21

"Victory Is in My Grasp!"

Okay.

I'd made it back to Olympus. That was originally the first part of my plan. Now I just had to not get immediately smited.

Zeus stood at the gates, radiating power.

Behind him, darkened clouds pulsed. Bolts of golden lightning bounced erratically. By this time, the other gods had started walking through the gates.

Hera. Poseidon. Athena. Ares.

All of them watching. Waiting.

I cleared my throat.

"Wow, what a surprise! Fancy seeing you all here."

No one laughed.

Great. Tough crowd.

Zeus took one thunderous step forward.

The cloud beneath me rumbled.

"You were banished."

I held up my hands.

"Okay, yes. But in my defense—"

"You were forbidden to return," he continued.

"Right, right. But technically, I didn't walk back in. I got delivered."

The comment caused his face to twist in confusion. Poseidon, who was just strolling up, pointed above them, "He has a point."

Hera elbowed him.

Zeus's eyes burned with electricity.

"Do you take me for a fool, boy?"

I shrugged, kicking a pebble of cloud.

"I mean...?"

A bolt of lightning slammed down at my feet, and I jumped back.

"Whoa! Okay! You're mad. Got it."

Behind Zeus, the other gods whispered among themselves. I could only catch snippets...

"Why is he back?"

"Did he summon that thing?"

"Wasn't he supposed to be on Earth forever?"

And that's when I saw the opening. They weren't just mad. They were uncertain.

I straightened up. Time for maximum confidence mode.

"You think I wanted to come back?" I scoffed. "Please. I had Earth under control."

Zeus glared.

"Then why are you here?"

I grinned.

"I was brought here," I said. "By something bigger than Olympus."

The murmurs grew louder.

Aphrodite raised an eyebrow.

"Bigger than Olympus?"

"Yeah," I said, arms wide. "Something that watches us."

A heavy silence fell. This was the first time I'd ever seen the gods not know how to respond.

Even Zeus hesitated.

And that's when I knew.

I had them.

Clasping my hands behind my back, I began pacing.

"Oh, don't mind me," I said. "I'm just a humble god of mischief. But when I got to Earth? Strange things started happening. I was being... watched."

In a theatrical flourish, I spun my arms, taking in the area.

Hera's face crinkled into a look of disbelief.

"By who?"

Grabbing my chin, I acted like I was pondering her question.

"That is the key piece of missing information, isn't it?"

More murmurs. Was this working?

Zeus hadn't fried me yet.

Maybe, just maybe, I could flip this whole thing in my favor.

I turned back to Zeus.

"You wanted me gone because you thought I was a menace."

Zeus slowly traced the beginnings of a new bolt of lightning, "You are."

"Sure, sure," I waved him off. "But what if I was banished at exactly the wrong time? What if my punishment…" I paused for dramatic effect. "…was a mistake?"

The murmuring swelled. Some gods actually looked concerned. Even Ares was considering my words. I had one chance. One shot to turn this around. Lifting my chin, I took a deep breath.

"Maybe, just maybe… I belong here after all."

No one said a word and for a second, I thought maybe I'd actually did it. I'd won. Tricked them all. They were putty in my hands.

Then Zeus waved his hand, and I realized how badly I'd miscalculated.

The sky split open.

Lightning crashed down around me.

The wind howled.

And Zeus's voice shook the heavens.

"ENOUGH."

My heart jumped into my throat.

Zeus was clearly done listening. He wasn't debating anymore. He wasn't considering my words. He was sending me back.

I scrambled.

"Wait! Hold on—"

Too late.

Zeus clenched his fist. Power crackled through the ground, and my world exploded in light.

When my senses finally stopped reeling, all I could feel was the wind whistling through my clothes and the distinct chill of stratospheric winds.

I was falling back toward Earth.

Fast.

Chapter 22
"Zeus Is Waiting"

Falling through the sky is not as fun as it sounds. Especially when you're getting thrown out of Olympus like a defective lightning bolt. Clouds rushed past me. The air screamed in my ears.

And somewhere above, I could still hear Zeus's voice ringing in my head.

"You have learned nothing."

The words hit harder than the fall. This was the same guy who once spent an entire afternoon teaching me how to split a storm in half, then ruffled my hair and called me "kiddo" when I finally got it right. Hearing that same voice act like I was just a broken lightning bolt stung way worse than I wanted to admit.

Kevin once asked me what it felt like to fall from Olympus.

At the time, I told him, "Like an extreme sport."

Going through it a second time, I realize my analysis was incorrect. It's more like getting launched out of a godly cannon. Spinning through the sky while rethinking every life choice. Hitting the ground with a force that should absolutely break all your bones ... but somehow doesn't.

This time I tried to brace for impact. I tried to direct the flow of static electricity to lessen the impact, but it was too late.

I slammed into the Earth.

Hard.

The ground shook. Birds fled the trees.

For a few seconds, all I could do was lie there, facedown in a crater. Stars danced in my vision. My body ached.

And the worst part?

I swore I could hear Kevin's voice in my ear.

"Duuuuude," he whispered. "That. Was. AWESOME!"

Carlos's voice followed.

"He's not dead, right?"

"I dunno. Poke him."

I half swatted in the voice's direction.

"Do not poke me," I slurred.

The voices disappeared.

Then...

Something oddly stick-like jabbed me in the ribs.

I rolled onto my back, swinging to get whatever it was away from me, only to find Kevin now standing over me, grinning like a maniac. I turned away and found Carlos looked deeply unimpressed.

"Welcome back," he said flatly.

I sat up slowly. Everything hurt. My divine energy was basically fried.

And I was back on Earth. In the mortal world. Stuck. Again.

Kevin clapped a hand on my shoulder.

"Welp. That didn't work."

I stared at him.

"Oh, really? I hadn't noticed."

Carlos tossed me a sucker.

"So. What now?"

I tried taking a deep breath. The bruising from the crash caused me to exhale a lot sooner than I'd wanted.

Carlos reached down, helping to pull me up.

"Alright," I said, brushing dirt off my jacket. "New plan."

Carlos raised an eyebrow.

"Another escape attempt?"

I grinned.

"Nope. Something better."

Kevin leaned forward.

"Do we get to commit arson?"

Carlos smacked him in the back of the head.

"What is wrong with you?"

The sound of them bickering behind me widened my smile. They had been there for me since I'd arrived. Even now, they were the first faces I saw upon returning.

Taking a few wobbly steps, I continued to dust myself. Zeus had dropped me on Morgan's Hill, a bluff that looked out over the small city. Taking in the view, I smirked.

"No more running. No more sneaking around."

I spread my arms.

"This place..."

The smirk now spread into a full-blown grin.

"It's mine now."

Carlos blinked.

"Excuse me?"

Kevin gasped.

"OH. MY. GOSH. ARE YOU TAKING OVER THE SCHOOL?"

I turned toward them. Blue sparks, leaping between my fingertips.

"Better," I said.

"I'm making it my Olympus."

Chapter 23

Chapter 23
"The Most Epic Smackdown Ever" (Almost)

L et's get one thing straight.

I didn't lose.

I just... didn't win.

The next day at school, I stood atop the bleachers, hands on my hips, looking down at my new kingdom. Since everyone was so insistent on my remaining on earth, I would claim the mortal world as my own. No Olympus? No problem.

I was going to make my new kingdom.

Kevin bounced on his heels.

"So, uh. What's the first decree of the new Olympus?"

Carlos found a log to sit on, pulling out another lollipop.

"This is ridiculous."

Kevin ignored him.

"We should make gym class illegal."

Carlos waggled the sucker in his direction, "We cannot make gym class illegal."

"Fine. But what if we..."

A thunderclap shattered the sky, stopping his next statement. The clouds turned gold as wind whipped around us. I grabbed Carlos and Kevin's shoulders to brace myself, but I also had a bad feeling about this.

Lightning continued to erupt, and a towering figure descended from the clouds. Draped in cloud soft robes, wreathed in stormlight, Zeus appeared.

King of the gods.

And my eternal pain in the butt dad.

He landed with enough force to crack the pavement.

Mortals? Frozen in place.

Kevin? Freaking out.

Carlos? Holding his head in his hands.

And me?

I straightened, defiantly walking down the bleacher steps.

"Oh, now you care about what I'm doing?"

Zeus's voice rumbled across the sky.

"Mintavious Olemar Johaneson."

I winced.

"Oof. Full name. That's never good."

His eyes burned with divine power.

"You dare call yourself a god?"

I gestured around.

"I mean... yeah? Seems pretty fitting."

A bolt of lightning slammed down in front of me.

Kevin screamed, and Carlos yanked at my arm.

"Mint. Shut up."

I shook him off.

"Oh, come on. He won't actually..."

Next thing I know, everything exploded. The world blurred. One second, I was standing. The next?

I was soaring backward at Mach Zeus.

I slammed into a building, the wall cracking on impact. Dust from shattered concrete floofed around me.

"Ow," I coughed.

Carlos rushed over.

"Mint! You good bro?"

Kevin peeked over the rubble.

"You really are a superhuman! That was epic."

I groaned. "Yeah, yeah. Super fun."

I forced myself back to my feet, my dad already barreling towards me.

I barely dodged his next strike, electricity ripping past my head. The ground split beneath my feet.

This wasn't like before; Dad wasn't just mad, he was done playing.

And the stupid part?

Some tiny piece of me still wanted him to stop, look at the mess I'd made down here, and say, *"You handled it. I'm proud of you."*

Instead, all I saw in his eyes was storm.

Rolling to my feet, I tried to summon my own lightning.

Tried to fight back.

But my divine power was too weak. There was no way it could compete against his, but there was one thing that I did better than anyone else…

I could do something stupid.

Grinning, I planted my feet, fists raised.

"You wanna go, old man?" I spat on the broken rubble. "Let's do this."

I charged straight at him.

Kevin grabbed his head, pulling his hair, "Has he lost his mind?!?"

I threw everything I had into one last, godly strike.

Lightning exploded from my fist.

Power crashed into the sky.

And for one, single, beautiful moment, I thought I actually had a chance.

But Zeus didn't flinch; he merely swatted me away. Crashing back into the ground, my brain felt like soup. My body ached as I lay there in the dirt, breathing heavy. Dad and his 'Almighty lightning' flashed above me. I was about to get obliterated.

I took a deep breath, stared intensely, mustered all the bravado I could, and at the top of my lungs screamed, "I regret nothing!"

Chapter 24
"I Am TRICKSTRIKE!" (No One Cares)

So maybe I lost. But that didn't mean I wasn't going down without style.

I groaned, dragging myself upright. Dust filled the air. My jacket was torn. My body felt like I'd been hit by a celestial freight train. Which, honestly, wasn't too far off. But I was still standing. And if I were standing, I could still talk smack.

Kevin whispered from behind a mailbox. "Boss... maybe just lay low this time?"

Carlos hissed, "Mint, do NOT..."

Too late.

I posed, spreading my arms, before taking a deep, luxurious bow.

"BEHOLD!" I declared. "I AM TRICKSTRIKE. GOD OF MISCHIEF AND LIGHTNING!"

Silence.

The wind whistled.

Somewhere in the distance, a car alarm went off.

Zeus just... stared.

Carlos palmed his face.

Kevin, bless his chaotic little soul, started clapping; "Stop that..." Carlos immediately slapped his hands down. "You trying to get us killed?"

Exasperated, Zeus exhaled deeply, releasing the energy he'd been storing for his next action.

"Enough," he rumbled.

"Pfft. What, tired already?"

His eyes sparked.

I gulped. Shooting him with finger guns.

"Haha. Kidding. Love you, Dad."

The thunder never stopped rolling overhead. I could feel the power he'd released building around Zeus.

This was it.

The final smite.

I was about to get erased from existence...or at the very least a stay-cation in Tartarus for a few millennia.

Honestly, that would've been a pretty epic way to go.

But a new voice cut through the storm.

"ZEUS ... OLD FRIEND."

Every instinct in me told me to freeze, because this wasn't a voice you ignored. It was ancient, sharp as a blade, and cold as the void. The kind of voice that stopped the world. Even Zeus stiffened.

The storm stilled. The clouds shifted. And from the sky....they arrived. This wasn't a god or a titan. At least not one that I knew. This being was something much, much older.

Zeus turned, his expression unreadable.

Kevin whispered, "Uh. Boss? Who are they?"

"No clue."

All I knew was that anyone who could make my dad pause mid-smite was not someone to underestimate.

Chapter 25

"Okay, Maybe I'm Stuck Here for a While"

When you shock the King of the Gods into silence, you know something big just happened. And for once, I wasn't the one who did it.

Zeus's eyes narrowed, the storm above us settling into an eerie calm. He turned toward the newcomer, shoulders squared like a warrior preparing for battle.

I, meanwhile, was trying to casually crawl away when Carlos grabbed me by the collar of my jacket.

"Nope."

"C'mon, man." I whispered. "I've been through a lot today."

Carlos just pointed at Zeus and I sighed.

"Fine. Staying. Watching."

The figure from the sky descended slowly, as if it was enjoying the spectacle it had caused. Even the air around them felt different.

Kevin hissed, "Dude. Are we about to witness a GOD FIGHT?"

Carlos threw his hands up, "I give up. You all just don't know when to shut your mouths, do you??"

I, personally, was still considering running.

But curiosity?

Curiosity won.

The figure stopped a few feet away. Their features were shadowed, shifting like mist. Their eyes though, were unmoving, unblinking. They reminded me of something, but I just couldn't put my finger on it. They were clearly watching everything. Then their eyes settled on me and the mist, where a mouth would normally be, contorted into some twisted facsimile of a smile.

Zeus spoke first.

"You overstep."

The figure's eyes shifted back towards him, "Do I?"

Every single godly instinct in my body screamed at me to shut up. So, naturally...I opened my mouth.

"So, uh," I said, stepping forward. "Not to interrupt the cryptic staring contest, but who exactly are you?"

The figure's head snapped back and the temperature dropped twenty degrees around me.

"You couldn't just... Nevermind. I don't know why I try with you sometimes. Do you even think before you let things come out of that thick skull of yours?" Carlos spat, his teeth rattling from the fifty-degree breeze. Kevin let out a tiny squeak.

The figure gave a knowing smile. Like I'd just proven them right.

"You already know."

I blinked.

"...I do?"

Because newsflash? I did not.

The figure chuckled, nodded back at my dad, and vanished.

Zeus finally released the tension in his shoulders, but his expression remained grim.

I watched him for a second, waiting for a comment. Realizing I wouldn't be getting one, I clapped my hands once.

"Soooo... we just gonna ignore that?"

For about five minutes Zeus stared at me.

"You are staying here."

Throwing my hands up, I pointed to where the being was just floating above them.

"Dad? Are you kidding me? Did we both not just see that... thing? Are you still going to ignore the shadow b..."

And that was when I remembered where I'd seen those eyes. The shadow beast that I had summoned, the Helios guard dog, had eyes that were similar to his. Same powers, same cold shifting shadows.

"Helios?" I whispered to myself.

Zeus's voice rumbled like distant thunder.

"Until we learn what watches you, Mint Johnson... you are Earth's problem now."

With that finality, he ascended in a bolt of lightning and the skies returned to their proper state.

"LET'S GOOO! MINT'S STUCK WITH US!" Kevin screamed.

It wasn't until now that I realized that all of the people around us had been frozen in time, the buzz of the student body returning to my senses. Or had we been removed from the stream of time?

Carlos continued rubbing warmth back into his arms.

"This is the worst day of my life."

Staring into the sky, my mind raced to process what had just occurred.

"Great," I muttered, "I'm grounded on Earth."

Chapter 26

"Define Behave..?"

I guess now I'm stuck on Earth... indefinitely.

That was annoying.

But you know what?

That doesn't mean I had to act like I was stuck.

I turned to Carlos and Kevin.

"Alright, listen up," I said, brushing off my jacket. "New plan."

Kevin bounced on his toes, "Oh yeah."

Smirking, I motioned for them to follow.

"If I'm gonna be trapped here, I might as well make this place fun."

Carlos pinched the bridge of his nose, "Meaning...???"

Placing my arms over their shoulders, I pulled them close.

"It means I'm taking over."

"Like a villain?" Kevin gasped.

"No Kev. He means like a menace." Carlos retorted.

Letting them go I walked between them, pointing at Kevin.

"More like a god. A divine presence. A force of chaos and entertainment."

"You mean a problem," Carlos huffed.

"You mean, more dangerous antics in which we..." he now waved a hand between himself and Kevin, "...will be pulled into?"

I winked, "Same thing."

"THIS IS THE BEST DAY OF MY LIFE!" Kevin yelled, running around in a circle.

"This is gonna be a disaster," Carlos said, walking off towards the school.

"Look. I'm not gonna, like, enslave humanity or anything. That sounds exhausting. But a few harmless tricks? A little divine influence? Yeah. That could be fun."

Carlos spun around in front of me.

"Mint. No."

Kevin grabbed my arm, "Mint. Yes."

Grinning, I again pulled them under my wings of mischief.

"Boys," I said. "Welcome to the era of Trickstrike."

Carlos stared at me.

"Mint," he said slowly.

"Yes, Carlos?"

"...What does that mean?"

I clapped his shoulder.

"It means," I said, "we're about to have some fun."

Chapter 27
"I Need a New Plan for Godhood"

Conquering Earth outright might not be an option. I say "might" because I haven't ruled it out completely. But being a god? That's still on the table. I just needed a new angle of attack.

A few days later, while sitting at our usual lunch tabl,e Carlos leered at me over his juice bottle.

"I hate this already."

Kevin pumped his fist.

"LET'S GOOO."

"See? Kevin gets it," I chuckled.

Carlos waved off the encouragement, "No. The only thing Kevin gets is an extra side of mashed potatoes, which seems to be replacing what few brain cells he has left."

Kevin paused mid-scoop of mashed potatoes and placed his spork down, trying to look distinguished.

"Alright. Let's break it down. Gods have or need three things: Power, Recognition, and Fear."

Carlos squinted, "I feel like one of those is not a requirement."

Kevin shrugged, "Nah, fear's legit. Name one god that isn't terrifying."

Carlos thought for a second.

"Aphrodite?"

Kevin rolled his eyes.

"Yeah, okay, but you know she could ruin your life in like five seconds."

Carlos nodded sagely, "True, true."

Refocusing them, I continued.

"So. Power is... currently questionable."

Carlos stared at me.

"Understatement."

I ignored him.

"Recognition? Not quite there yet."

Again, Carlos stared.

"Also an understatement."

"Fear?" I shrugged. "Eh. We can work on that."

This tim,e Carlos tossed a nugget at my face.

"MINT."

Kevin snapped his fingers.

"What if we make you a cult?"

Carlos whirled on him.

"WHAT?"

Kevin grinned.

"Y'know. Like, build a following. Get some loyal subjects."

Carlos paled.

"Kevin, we are not starting a cult."

Kevin held up his hands.

"Relax! I'm just brainstorming."

I pointed at him.

"I like where your head's at."

"Of course you do," Carlos groaned.

Standing, I looked around the cafeteria.

"The way I see it, this is going to be a three-pronged process."

"And here we go..." Carlos deadpanned.

Enthusiastic as ever, Kevin dug through his backpack for a notebook.

"What do you have in mind boss?

I turned on my heel.

"One: Get the mortals to believe in me."

"Two: Establish divine authority."

"Three: Make sure Zeus doesn't smite me back into the Stone Age."

Carlos squinted.

"That third one really should be number one."

Kevin nodded.

"Yeah, that guy seems really committed to smiting you."

I waved them off.

"Details."

Carlos sighed.

"No, Mint. That's not a detail. That's life and death."

I shrugged.

"Eh. I've lived through worse."

Carlos gestured wildly.

"HAVE YOU?"

"Okay, okay, but I like this plan." Kevin grinned, "But where do we start?"

I thought about it, tapping my chin. A million thoughts flooding my mind. One in particular caused the largest Cheshire grin to form.

"Oh," I said.

"I know exactly where to start."

Chapter 28

"The School Is Now My Olympus"

If I couldn't go back to Olympus, then I'd do the next best thing. I'd make my own. And where better to start than school? You know, the place where I'm already considered a menace to society.

Carlos dragged a hand down his face.

"Mint, no. We cannot do this."

Kevin prodded with feigned devious innocence, "Boss, we can easily pull this off."

Carlos spun on him.

"STOP ENCOURAGING HIM!"

I climbed on top of a cafeteria table and cupped my mouth,

"Students of this fine institution! May I have your attention!"

The entire lunchroom went silent, their eyes turning towards me. Even the lunch lady stopped mid-scoop.

Good.

I had their attention.

I cleared my throat.

"I come before you today with a proposal."

Carlos hissed. "Oh my gods, please stop."

I ignored him.

"This school needs order. This school needs leadership."

I threw out my arms.

"This school needs... a god. And lucky for you," I added, forcing a grin, "the original one got kicked out of his old job."

If Olympus didn't want me, fine.

I'd just build my own pantheon out of mortals, neon lights, and cafeteria pizza.

Silence.

Then, from the bac,k a single voice coughed.

"Bro, what??"

Kevin clapped dramatically.

"YES. ALL HAIL MINT."

From another corne, I heard, "Why is he standing on the table?"

Some freshmen nearby chuckled, "Is this a joke?"

Carlos just laid his head down on the table.

I raised my hands.

"I know, I know," I said, "This is a lot to take in. But hear me out."

Step One: Get the mortals to believe in me.

Time to sell myself.

"Have I not performed miracles?" I asked.

"Have I not defied the very laws of nature?"

"Did I not zap the vending machine and bestow free snacks upon you all?"

A murmur spread through the crowd. The vending machine stunt was already legendary. They remembered.

Good.

I had them.

Now to seal the deal.

I gestured grandly.

"What if I told you—" I paused for dramatic effect. "I could do MORE?"

"Oooooooh," Kevin flickered jazz hands in front of me.

Reaching down I picked up the slice of pizza from my tray.

Someone in the back yelled, "That's just cafeteria pizza."

Holding it out like the Excalibur of questionable cheese.

"Ah," I said. "But what if it was BETTER?"

A crackle of electricity.

A spark of power.

I channeled a little bit of my energy and BOOM.

The pizza glowed.

Overhead, the fluorescent lights flickered in perfect sync, a stutter that had nothing to do with old wiring.

Gasps rippled through the cafeteria.

Across the room I heard, "No way."

" Will you stop doing magic in public?" Carlos said, tugging at my pants leg.

Stepping down, I handed the slice to our schools self proclaimed foodie. Skeptically, she took a bite, chewed, then nodded in approval.

"Divine," she declared, and the lunchroom erupted.

People surged forward.

Kevin scrambled atop the table, pointing at me.

"THE FOOD GOD HAS ARRIVED."

Step One?

Complete.

Chapter 29
"Naturally, I Declare a Prank War"

It had been a few weeks and no complaints had occurred. Kevin thought it best I only 'blessed" a certain number of food items a day, and that seemed to keep the people happy. With my divine rule established, it was time to cement my legacy. And what better way to announce my reign than with an unprecedented act of chaos? A challenge. A test of wit and mischief. A prank war.

Carlos looked like he had aged ten years.

"Mint. You can't just declare a prank war."

Kevin, ever my right-hand man, was already rubbing his hands together.

"Oh, he absolutely can."

"I refuse to be a part of this," Carlos said, shaking his head.

Kevin clapped him on the shoulder.

"Too late, buddy. We're all in this together."

I climbed atop a nearby lunch table, which was quickly becoming my preferred throne.

"Let it be known," I announced, voice carrying across the cafeteria, "from this moment forth, all who walk these halls shall be subject to the greatest test of trickery ever devised."

Kevin pumped his fist.

"PRANK WAR!"

The room exploded into whispers and excitement.

Naturally, not everyone was on board. Someone from the chess club squinted at me.

"Is there a prize?"

I winked in their direction.

"Honor. Bragging rights. The respect of your peers."

No one said anything.

"Fine. The winner gets a free item from the vending machine daily for a month."

The cafeteria exploded in cheers.

"You realize this is going to end badly, right?" Carlos protested.

Waving my hands, I dismissed the thought.

"All great wars have casualties."

Carlos stared at me.

"This is a prank war, Mint. No one's actually dying."

I looked away.

"No one's died... yet."

I could see the frustration boiling on his face as he reached for another sucker.

Kevin leaned in. "So, what's the first move, O Mighty Trickstrike?"

A thin smile crossed my lips.

"Simple."

And that's how the entire sophomore class walked into third-period math to find every chair mysteriously glued to the ceiling.

The uproar was instantaneous.

But the energy..

For a second, chalk dust hung in the air like it was stuck mid-fall, and my skin buzzed with the same caged-storm feeling I'd had when Zeus locked down my powers. This wasn't just tape and glue anymore; my tricks were starting to lean on the kind of energy Olympus usually kept under lock and key.

Students pointed and laughed. The math teacher just stood in the doorway, blinking.

Casually, I entered and sat in my assigned seat and started sipping on a juice box. The only seat remaining on the floor.

Mission. Accomplished.

I expected retaliation, but how else was I supposed to start a school-wide prank war?

During gym class, I opened my locker to grab my shoes, only to find them replaced with loaves of bread.

Just... bread.

Someone had actually gone through the trouble of unbagging and framing two loaves of bread to look like shoes. Soggy, bready shoes. It was equal parts impressive and unsettling.

"I'm almost proud," Carlos quipped from over my shoulder.

By lunchtime, the entire school was divided into teams. It was my loyal followers versus the resistance.

Kevin made battle plans on the back of a history worksheet, while Carlos droned on about how this would all fall apart. By the end of the day, the school had descended into a full-blown strategic operation.

Chalk exploded from erasers.

Lockers mysteriously played recorded dolphin noises.

One hallway became a slip-and-slide.

And somewhere, somehow, a mysterious bucket of glitter sat ominously above the principal's door.

By midday, the fire alarms had false-triggered twice, the PA system kept crackling with static, and the lights in the main hall blinked in a slow, creepy rhythm that made everyone glance up.

I could feel that unseen attention again, like the school itself had become a little Olympus, and someone somewhere was taking notes.

When Carlos found out about the bucket, he pulled me aside.

"This is going to end with you in detention, isn't it?"

Maniacally rubbing my hands together, I beamed with pride.

"Not if I win first."

"Mint," Carlos said quietly, "this isn't just about pranks anymore. The whole building freaks out every time you sneeze electricity."

I shrugged it off.

Better to pretend I didn't hear the fear in his voice ...or the low hum in the vents that answered it.

Chapter 30

"Okay, So Maybe Humans Are Kinda Cool"

J ust this once, I'll admit it.

Maybe—maybe—humans aren't entirely useless.

I mean, sure. They can't summon lightning, they don't have divine reflexes, and they're terrible at reading the room. But when it comes to causing absolute, glorious mayhem?

They've got potential.

The prank war was still raging three weeks later. I thought the majority of the student population would have just rolled over. I never expected a full-scale resistance. At this point, it wasn't just a few students messing around; it was organized chaos. There were alliances. Secret hideouts. Smuggling rings for whoopee cushions and disappearing ink. This wasn't just pranks anymore. It was a truly masterful war.

Kevin had taken the role of my general.

"Alright," he said, sprawled over a cafeteria bench, mapping out enemy positions. "We lost ground in the science wing after the principal banned water balloons."

Carlos rubbed his temples.

"That's because Mint threw one at him!"

"Allegedly," I corrected.

Carlos looked exhausted.

"What even is the goal here?"

Kevin threw his arms up.

"Victory."

Carlos squinted.

"Victory in what?"

Kevin replied with a single word, "Yes."

Meanwhile, the Resistance, a.k.a. the people who dared challenge my divine rule, was led by the most unexpected person ever.

Travis Mason.

A junior Honor Roll student on the soccer team who didn't talk much. You'd think he'd be above the chaos.

Nope.

Dude took one whoopee cushion to the chair, and now he was on a warpath.

Our latest battle was during gym class.

Dodgeball.

Which, for once, wasn't just a game. No, no. This was a showdown. Team captains, Me versus Travis. The fate of our prank kingdoms on the line. Kevin rubbed my shoulders, hyping me up.

"Boss, if you lose, we surrender everything."

"Or we could just... not do this?" Carlos grunted.

I wasn't listening. This had stopped being about reason a long time ago. My respect as a god of mischief was on the line.

The game began. Balls flew everywhere. Students yelled, ducked, dived. Chaos. Pure perfect Chaos.

Kids were being tagged out left and right. Vendettas from the previous week's pranks were being avenged. By the last few minutes of class, it had come down to the final duel.

Me and Travis.

A ball in each of our hands.

The gym fell silent, eyes darting back and forth between us. Travis narrowed his eyes, and with all the smug cheekiness I had cultivated, I stuck my thumbs in my ears, waggled my hands, and stuck out my tongue.

"Come on Travis. You want my kingdom? You're gonna have to take it from me!"

A flash of understanding passed between us.

A truce?

A final warning?

A moment of respect?

No.

The whistle blew to start the round, and we both threw at the same time.

My ball whizzed through the air.

His did the same.

Everything slowed.

The world held its breath.

POW!

The balls collided midair, popping under the pressure. Not like actual explosions, but they had been booby-trapped with glitter. So the entire gymnasium got covered in gold, pink, blue, and purple sparkles.

Noone spoke for a moment, then Kevin pulled out his phone, taking a zillion pictures.

"WORTH IT."

Coach Wilson, covered in glitter and disappointment, sighed.

"Detention. All of you."

Travis and I locked eyes and burst out laughing.

In that moment, it hit me. Humans might be a mess. They may not have the best perspectives on how their lives should be lived, but when it comes to pulling off stupid, reckless, hilarious stunts?

Yeah.

They're kinda awesome.

I suppose the idea of returning to Olympus no longer felt like the only win condition.

Chapter 31

"Until They Betray Me"

Let me tell you something.

Nothing, and I mean NOTHING, ruins a perfect reign of chaos faster than a snitch, and that's exactly what happened. Someone...some traitor...ratted me out.

Now, don't get me wrong. I knew this prank war wasn't gonna last forever, but I expected to go out in glory. One final, grand act of mischief before the school collapsed into awe and legend. Instead? I got sold out.

Kevin paced the cafeteria.

"Who did it? Who turned on us?"

Carlos looked up from his phone.

"All of you turned on yourselves the moment this started."

I folded my arms.

"Carlos, not now. We're investigating."

Waving his hands, he gestured at the random scattering of notebook paper and school maps.

"Investigating what? It was OBVIOUSLY you! You've been on every security camera since day one!"

I blinked.

"...They have cameras?"

Carlos looked ready to scream. Kevin kept pacing.

"Let's go over the facts." He smacked a notebook onto the table.

"When did you start taking notes?" Carlos frowned.

Kevin flipped through the pages. "Day one, boss. This was history in the making."

I nodded in approval.

Carlos stared at both of us.

"I need new friends."

But back to the real issue. Somebody had spilled EVERYTHING to the teachers. Now the entire school was on lockdown.

No more pranks.

No more carefully placed buckets of pudding.

No more glitter bombs.

There were new signs on the doors, extra staff roaming the halls, and a couple of strangers in suits checking the breaker panels like the building itself was under investigation. Every time the lights flickered, they wrote something down on their clipboards. I didn't need divine senses to know they weren't here for regular school drama.

The war was over.

Not only had I been sentenced to a week of detention... I was the ONLY ONE sentenced.

Unacceptable.

Back on Olympus, when I got punished, everyone knew it was because I'd gone bigger than anyone else.

Here, it felt different.

Like somebody had pointed a giant arrow at me and whispered, *That one. That's the one you want.*

Being the only name on the detention slip didn't feel like justice. It felt like a setup.

And yeah, fine, it also felt... bad.

These were *my* people now, my school, my chaos crew, and somebody in the middle of all that had decided I was better off alone on the chopping block.

I tapped my fingers on the lunch table.

"Alright. We find the rat, expose them, and deliver sweet justice."

"Mint, this is not a crime drama." Carlos vented.

Our first lead came a few days later. Kevin's phone had been buzzing sporadically, intel from his network of spies. This time though, his eyes went wide.

"Guys."

He turned his screen toward us, where a single message on the school's anonymous gossip site read...

"Mint's reign is over. He had it coming."

"A CONSPIRACY!?" Kevin gasped.

Ever the pragmatist, Carlos lowered Kevin's hand from his forehead.

"Or... and hear me out... people are just sick of you getting away with this."

I squinted at the screen. The betrayal stung. Not because I got caught, but because someone actually thought they could outmaneuver me.

Kevin leaned in.

"How are we gonna handle this boss?"

To which Carlos immediately chimed.

"The move is doing NOTHING. There is no move."

Cupping my chin I pondered momentarily.

"No, no. We retaliate."

Carlos groaned. "Against WHO?" Carlos moaned. "You don't even know who did it!"

Chapter 32

"Fine, I'll Be a Hero or Whatever"

Revenge could wait.

I mean, don't get me wrong. I was still 100% finding out who snitched. But it seems I had bigger problems.

It started right after detention.

There I was, minding my own business, plotting my glorious comeback, when suddenly a loud crash rang through the hall, followed by screaming.

Kevin and Carlos froze.

"...That didn't sound good," Carlos said, grimacing.

Kevin brushed past hi,m trying to reach the door first.

"Or it sounded very good."

"That didn't sound like a prank explosion, genius. That might be an actual problem."

Eyebrows raised, I followed Kevin, "Or an opportunity."

We ran to the hallway, where a catastrophe was already in full swing. Locker doors hung off their hinges. Singed posters wafted to the floor. And in the center of it all, a monster stood towering in the middle of the Art wings intersection.

"So... we all see that, right?" Kevin blinked.

Carlos sighed. "Unfortunately."

It was big. Seven feet tall, glowing eyes, too many teeth. It looked like it had crawled out of a nightmare. Or, more likely, an accidental summoning gone wrong.

"I would like the record to show that I have not committed any summonings since that last fiasco! This one isn't on me."

The monster snarled as students ran screaming in every direction.

Teachers? Nowhere in sight.

Kevin rapped his fingers against each other.

"Alright, boss. What's the move?"

Carlos grabbed my sleeve, "The move is running."

Shaking him off, I pulled them around a corner, analyzing the creature.

"Absolutely not. This is my school."

Carlos blinked incredulously.

"I'm sorry? I thought you hated it here?"

I did. Or I thought I did.

But the idea of that thing tearing through Kevin's dumb conspiracy notebook, or smashing Carlos into a locker, or crashing through Mom-Energy-Lady's front yard made my stomach knot in a way even freefall never had.

"Yeah, but I hate getting upstaged more."

We must not have moved fast enough, because the beast snapped its head toward us, it's eyes locking onto me.

Carlos tensed.

"Uuuhh, Mint? It's looking at you."

"That makes sense. You were pretty loud," Kevin panted, leaning further back against the lockers.

Cracking my knuckles, I waved for them to follow. "Alright, let's do this."

Carlos groaned.

"Oh, for the love of..."

Now the idea was that we charge it, surprising the creature into a stunned submission.

I guess it didn't get the memo.

Just as we rounded the corner, it was halfway down the hall and almost on top of us. I barely had time to dodge before claws slashed the air where my head had been. The thing was fast.

Claws tore through the brick walls, sending debris scattering. Clearly, it didn't lack in the strength department, which meant I was going to have to get creative.

Skiddings from that last dodge, I spun to face it.

"DO YOU HAVE A PLAN?" Kevin yelled.

"Of course," I winked.

Carlos yelled, "IS IT A GOOD PLAN?"

I hesitated.

"...Define good."

The monster lunged once more, and again I ducked, dove between its legs, and popped up behind it.

"Alright, buddy," I called. "Let's make a deal."

It turned toward me, growling.

Kevin whimpered as he hefted a trashcan above his head. "Boss, I don't think it negotiates."

"That's a shame," I gloated, "because I'm not asking."

Clapping my hands I tried to generate a spark of energy. I knew I still didn't have much, but a flicker was all I'd need.

The monster flinched at the sight, creating the opening I had been searching for. I launched myself forward, sliding under its massive arms.

ZAP.

I slapped my palms against its chest, channeling what little godly power I could conjure. There was a brief crackle of energy.

The beast howled and dissipated into a plume of smoke.

Gone.

There was silence for a good few moments before Kevin had to ruin it.

"ABSOLUTELY LEGENDARY!"

"What," Carlos said, voice dangerously calm, "was that?"

"A very, very bad summoning," I said sniffing the smoke particles on my shirt.

Carlos exhaled.

"Mint. Did you—"

"Irrelevant." I cut him off.

What concerned me was not the fact that I hadn't summoned the beast, but that it only took that tiny amount of power to cause it to return to its realm.

Students peeked from their hiding spots, many already whispering. From somewhere in the crowd ,a quizzical voice chimed.

"Yo. Did Mint just save the school?"

I blinked, and Kevin beamed with pride.

"Yes. Yes, he did!"

Carlos didn't even stop him for trying.

Another voice added, "Dude. That was actually kinda cool."

Then a third voice interjected, "I mean... he is a god, right?"

I stood there. Listening. Watching the whispers spread.

Was this what recognition felt like? Is this what the other gods felt when they received worship and prayers from their patrons?

Maybe being stuck here wasn't so bad after all.

Chapter 33
"One Last Escape Attempt"

Alright.

So I may have accidentally become a hero. Didn't plan on it. Didn't ask for it. But hey, sometimes fate just does its thing. That being said...

It's not like I'm staying.

No way.

No how.

I still had one last escape attempt up my sleeve.

Carlos threw up his hands.

"You JUST saved the school, and now you want to leave?"

"Exactly. Gotta exit while I'm on top."

Carlos looked like he wanted to strangle me.

I paced the cafeteria, hands behind my back like a criminal mastermind.

"Alright, boys. Every attempt before now? Amateur hour. But this? This is the one."

Kevin pouted like a whiny baby.

"You're really going to leave us?"

"Why do you keep entertaining this?" Carlos said, tapping a finger on the desk.

"Because it's fun," Kevin replied, giddy.

"This is why we can't have nice things," said Carlo,s putting his forehead on the table.

I turned to my most loyal accomplice.

"Kevin. Do we have the supplies?"

Kevin saluted.

"Sir, Everything's in place. Sir!"

Carlos raised a brow.

"You mean the supplies you somehow stole from science class?"

Kevin shrugged.

"Borrowed."

Carlos leaned back, arms folding over his chest.

"Do you plan on returning them?"

"Maybe…I mean, if there's anything left, sure why not?"

Carlos rubbed his temples.

Clasping my hands together I looked between them.

"Alright, gentlemen. Welcome to Operation Storm Surge."

"It has a name? Oh, this is about to get comically bad." Carlos laughed.

The objective?

Summon a storm big enough to open a portal back to Olympus.

No more baby lightning tricks.

No more half-powered sparks.

I needed a real, full-blown, earth-shaking thunderstorm. One way or another.

Kevin pulled out the schematics. Okay, fine. It was a messy notebook page covered in doodles and questionably accurate math; but the idea was solid.

Step 1:

Find the tallest point in town. Water tower? Radio tower? TBD.

Step 2:

Create an artificial lightning rod. Heavily inspired by "Frankenstein."

Step 3:

Summon the storm.

Carlos stared at the horrifyingly bad drawing.

"…You are actually insane."

Kevin leaned in.

"Boss. There's just one problem."

I raised a brow.

"Only one?"

"Okay, fine, a lot of problems. But mainly: how do we get a storm if Zeus is still blocking your powers?"

Carlos snapped his fingers.

"A rare moment of clarity from Kevin. That's a GREAT question, actually."

I waved him off.

"Zeus only blocks my godly power. Doesn't mean I can't jumpstart the process."

Carlos frowned.

"And how exactly do you plan on doing that?"

Mischievously, I pulled out a homemade rocket and Carlos' mouth dropped open.

"Wicked," Kevin gasped.

Carlos grabbed his hair.

"WHAT... IS ... THAT?"

"An experiment." I shrugged nonchalantly.

Carlos shook his head.

"No, that's a felony."

Look.

I had researched this.

In the most chaotic corners of the internet, I found an interesting fact:

Rocket-triggered lightning is totally a thing.

It's real. Scientists do it all the time.

So... if they can do it, why can't I?

Kevin was all in.

"This is it. This is the moment. We're about to make history."

Carlos grabbed my arm.

"This is the moment you go to PRISON."

I shook him off.

"Relax. What's the worst that could happen?"

Carlos began listing things, "Expulsion, jail time, DEATH."

Kevin wagged a scholarly finger, "But also immortality in the school legend books."

Carlos facepalmed.

"You are both beyond my help."

We planned to meet up under the cover of a completely normal Tuesday night. Making our way to the radio tower at the edge of town, I had a good feeling about the plan. The wind picked up. The air felt charged. It was perfect. Pulling out the rocket, I waited for Kevin to prepare. Holding up his phone he started the camera.

I'm recording this for future generations."

Carlos looked at us, dumbfounded as I lit the fuse.

FOOM.

The rocket soared into the sky on a perfect trajectory. I had aimed it straight toward the storm clouds forming overhead and waited. This was it. This was the moment I'd been waiting for.

And then—

CRACK-BOOM!

A lightning bolt shot down.

Striking not the rocket...

...but me.

For a blinding second, everything was white-hot.

Electricity pulsed through my veins.

I felt powerful.

Whole.

But when I opened my eyes.

Zeus was standing right in front of me.

Uh-oh.

Chapter 34
"It Worked... Sort Of"

First thought:

Ow.

Second thought:

Oh no.

Third thought:

Why is Dad looking at me like that?

Lightning still crackled around me. My hands tingled. My skin buzzed with energy. For the first time since I was banished, since Zeus stripped me of my powers, I felt like a god again.

And I was not the only one who noticed.

Zeus loomed over me, doing that glowing regal thing he always did when he was trying to impress someone. That pure, unchecked authority that he radiated while his toga fluttered in the wind and those thunderous eyes locked onto mine.

The storm rumbled overhead, skies vibrating with tension. And I, ever the master of tact and wisdom, said the smartest thing I could think of:

"Hey, Pops. Long time no see."

Kevin had tried to hide, but on top of the tower, there really wasn't anyplace to go.

"DUDE. RUN."

"OH, WE'RE SO DEAD," said Carlos, panicking.

"Nah," I said, "I think we're about to have a nice, father-son chat."

Zeus folded his arms, the winds dying down.

"Mintavious."

Ah, great. The Zeus Voice. Deep. Echoing. The kind of voice that makes entire civilizations rethink their life choices.

"So," I said casually, "what brings you to my humble kingdom?"

Zeus's eyebrow raised.

"You mean the radio tower you nearly destroyed?"

I snapped my fingers.

"Heh heh,right. That."

Carlos grabbed at my arm.

"MINT. READ THE ROOM."

Zeus tilted his head at the scene.

"You've been busy I see."

A lopsided smirk crossed my lips, "You know me. Always making an impression."

Zeus sighed, looking toward the school in the distance.

"The mortals speak of you," he said. "Some as a trickster. Others as a hero."

"What can I say? I'm multi-talented." I said, giving him spirit fingers.

Then Zeus's gaze hardened.

"But you are neither."

The clouds darkened once more.

Kevin whispered. "Oh, I do not like that tone."

Zeus floated forward.

"You were exiled for a reason," he said, hands opening in exasperation. "Do you understand why?"

Dismissively, I waved a hand.

"Something about 'reckless behavior' and 'almost collapsing the sky,' blah blah blah."

Zeus's expression darkened.

"It was about responsibility, Mint."

I raised a brow.

"Says the guy who threw me out of Olympus instead of teaching me."

Zeus fell momentarily silent.

At that, I had an epiphany.

I wasn't afraid of him anymore.

Before, standing in front of Zeus meant bowing. Shrinking. No one should have to do that to their own dad. Today, for some reaso,n was different. I'd stood my ground. I'd faced storms. I'd fought a monster.

I wasn't the same Thunderbrat I used to be.

Taking a step forward, I continued. No sarcasm, no wit. Just words I'd longed to speak to him for millennia.

"Look," I said. "I get it. You wanted to teach me a lesson. I know I'm not the most earnest kid, so I get it. But there are some other things I learned too. Some things I'm not sure if you were ready for me to understand."

Zeus raised an eyebrow.

"Oh?"

"Yeah," I said. "I learned that being a god is more than just throwing lightning bolts."

Zeus's face remained unreadable, so I kept going.

"Power's not just about having it," I said. "It's about what you do with it."

For a moment, Zeus just stared at me. Then, very slowly...he smiled.

This time it was Kevin's jaw that dropped.

"Oh, NOW he learns?" Carlos screamed, facepalming.

Zeus nodded.

"Perhaps exile wasn't a waste after all."

"Wait. What?" I sputtered.

Zeus snapped his fingers, a portal crackling open behind him. The ring hummed with divine energy. The way back to Olympus. It was open. Waiting.

Kevin grabbed my shoulders.

"DUDE. THIS IS IT. YOU'RE GOING BACK."

Carlos didn't say anything; he just pulled out a sucker and stuck it in his mouth.

I should've been excited.

I should've been rushing through that portal.

But instead...I hesitated.

Zeus noticed.

"You've earned your return," he said. "Come."

I looked back.

Back at the school.

At the humans.

At Kevin and Carlos.

And suddenly, I wasn't so sure I wanted to leave.

Chapter 35

"The Legend of Thunderbrat Begins"

The portal crackled behind Zeus; shimmering, hues of a golden aurora, humming with the energy of Olympus itself.

My way home.

A way back to my rightful place in the heavens.

And yet...

I wasn't moving.

Kevin nudged me.

"Dude. What are you waiting for?"

Carlos leaned against the rail, face extremely calm.

"Yeah. I thought this was your whole thing."

I didn't answer. In truth, I didn't know what I was waiting for. For months, all I wanted was to go back. To stand among the gods again. To reclaim my title. My power.

I looked at the portal... and I looked at the city below. My mind raced with images of the school. The chaos. The dumb, reckless, ridiculous humans. I had been so keen on running away from them, that I hadnt gotten to know them. Once I had, well...

Zeus watched me carefully.

"You hesitate," he said.

I scratched my head.

"Yeah, well... maybe I have a few questions."

Zeus nodded.

"Ask them."

That was way easier than I expected it to be. He usually is tight-lipped about everything. I stuffed my hands into my hoodie pocket.

"What happens if I step through?"

Zeus shrugged.

"You resume your place among the gods. You return to Olympus."

Kevin raised a hand.

"I'm sorry, Mr. Zeus sir, quick question? What if he stays?"

Zeus tilted his head.

"That is his decision."

Carlos' face almost lit up.

"Wait. He can stay?"

Zeus smirked.

"I never said he couldn't."

My eyes blinked several times. Did I just hear what I thought I did?

"Hold on. Are you telling me this whole time, I had a choice?"

Zeus' shoulders raised slightly, "Did you?"

I squinted.

"What kind of cryptic answer..."

Chuckling Zeus smiled.

"Loki's not the only mischievous one in the realm. Where did you think you got your talent from? I know you didn't think you got it from your mother?"

I was shocked, I'd never seen this side of dad. Before I could find my words he continued.

"I exiled you to learn, Mint. The lesson wasn't about punishment. It was about understanding who you are."

I thought about that. About everything that happened. The pranks. The failures. The humans I met. The storm I had survived. I thought about how I'd changed. How my time amongst the mortals ... had changed me.

Admitting it, even in my own head, was scarier than any fall. I was choosing a noisy, messy little city over endless power and golden clouds—and somehow it felt more right than anything I'd done as a "proper" god.

Glancing over my shoulder at Kevin and Carlos, it was all I could do to not burst into laughter.

"Alright, Pops," I said. "I think I figured it out."

Zeus raised an eyebrow.

"Oh have you now?"

I turned towards the city, arms outstretched.

"Yeah. Turns out, I kinda like it here."

"YES!" Kevin fist-pumped.

"Of course you do," Carlos half chuckled.

Zeus just nodded.

"I take it you've chosen then?"

Reaching out a hand I looked him straight in the eyes.

"Guess so."

He grasped my hand and I could feel a little of my powers return.

"Don't make me regret this kid."

Behind him the portal rippled, vanishing in a crack of thunder.

Kevin almost bowled me over in excitement. Carlos jus scratched his head and looked at me through a single cheery eye.

"I knew you were too stupid to leave."

"Well, first things first," I said, "If I'm gonna stay, I might as well do it right."

Kevin's eyes sparkled, "Meaning?"

I turned them both to face the school. My new kingdom. My Olympus. A place worthy of my divine influence.

"Meaning it's time to make a name for myself."

Zeus watched me laughing.

Loud, booming, and surprisingly genuine. Like tears in the corners of his eyes laughing.

"Then go, Trickstrike." he said, placing a hand on my shoulder, "Show the world who you really are."

My breath caught. Did he just call me...Trickstrike!

Not Mint? Not Thunderbrat?

A name of my own making.

My dad had finally accepted me as a true god of Olympus.

Chapter 36
"Diary Entry #1: I'm Not Done Yet"

Let's get one thing straight:

I regret nothing.

Not the exile.

Not the pranks.

Not the accidental monster summoning.

Not even the fact that Zeus nearly smote me into a pile of ash.

Because at the end of the day?

I won.

Seriously, think about it.

I got banished from Olympus for being a menace, took over a middle school in record time, and became a legend by accident. I mean seriously, who does that?

And instead of crawling back to Olympus like a good little god...I stayed. I made my choice.

I won't lie...it still freaks me out how easy that choice felt in the moment.

But I gotta say, I kinda like it here.

Sure, Olympus had power and luxury. Sure, it had golden palaces with ambrosia and lightning on demand.

But Earth?

Earth had mad chaos.

It had weird, unpredictable, messy humans who somehow made life more fun.

It had Kevin, and Carlos, and an entire school of poor unsuspecting fools who had no idea what's coming next.

It had opportunity.

And as of a few months ago, it officially had me "Full Time" Baby!

I mean, let's be honest.

I'm Mint Johnson.

I'm Trickstrike.

The Thunderbrat.

And I am just getting started.

Kevin says I should keep this journal thing going.

Carlos says I shouldn't.

Guess who I'm listening to?

Exactly.

So, diary or journal or whatever you are—get ready.

Because if you think this was wild?

Just wait until you see what I do next.

OHHHH...

Side Note to self:

Figure out who sent you that note last week. You know, the one with no name and no return address.

Just had a single line of text.

"You should have gone back..."